FLIGHT FROM THE TEMPLE

To
The Werts
Best Wishes!
Peter Reese Doyle
9/25/09

FLIGHT FROM THE TEMPLE

PETER REESE DOYLE

Tate Publishing & *Enterprises*

Flight From the Temple
Copyright © 2008 by Peter Reese Doyle. All rights reserved.

This title is also available as a Tate Out Loud product. Visit www.tatepublishing.com for more information.

No part of this publication may be reproduced, stored in a retrieval system or transmitted in any way by any means, electronic, mechanical, photocopy, recording or otherwise without the prior permission of the author except as provided by USA copyright law.

This novel is a work of fiction. Names, descriptions, entities and incidents included in the story are products of the author's imagination. Any resemblance to actual persons, events and entities is entirely coincidental.

The opinions expressed by the author are not necessarily those of Tate Publishing, LLC.

Published by Tate Publishing & Enterprises, LLC
127 E. Trade Center Terrace | Mustang, Oklahoma 73064 USA
1.888.361.9473 | www.tatepublishing.com

Tate Publishing is committed to excellence in the publishing industry. The company reflects the philosophy established by the founders, based on Psalm 68:11,
"The Lord gave the word and great was the company of those who published it."

Book design copyright © 2008 by Tate Publishing, LLC. All rights reserved.
Cover design by Leah LeFlore
Interior design by Lindsay B. Behrens

Published in the United States of America

ISBN: 978-1-60604-276-2
1. Fiction: Action & Adventure   2. Juvenile Fiction: Suspense/Thriller
08.07.10

FOR

ALEXANDRA ELISABETH PURVIS

DON'T TURN THE PAGE!

Don't turn the page!—There's danger here
From poisonous reptile, iron-tipped spear,
From falling walls, collapsing floors
And deadly traps past ancient doors!

All, all designed to keep away
The strangers who'd conspire to stray
In search of treasure—gems and gold—
Intruders brash and crass and bold
—Who'd dare to penetrate these halls
Of icy stone and treacherous walls,
To desecrate the sacred rooms
And violate the demons' tombs.

Don't turn the page!—There's danger here!
There's cause for trembling, flight, and fear
Of desperate men who will betray
All, all, whom they find in their way!
Great courage and great faith must be
The armor 'gainst this enemy,

For nothing less can bear the strain,
The dread, the turmoil, and the pain.

But Wait!—I know a Maiden Fair
Who's courage is beyond compare,
Whose heart can face the trials of life,
Whose spirit conquers fears and strife;
Who does not flinch nor turn away,
Who walks with faith the Narrow Way.
And then I knew this yarn might test—
But not dislodge her spirit's rest.

To this Sweet Girl I give this book,
And truly hope she'll take a look
And find some pleasure in the tale
Of youths whose courage did not fail.
May she enjoy—her whole life long—
The joys that come to Faith that's strong,
That does not shrink in danger's face—
This Girl of Kindliness and Grace.

TABLE OF CONTENTS

THE RAIDERS CONVERGE.................11
RETURN TO AFRICA 17
TO THE TEMPLE 27
TRAPPED 37
"WATCH FOR SNAKES!"..................45
"WHICH WAY?"........................53
"WE CAN'T GO BACK!"..................61
"WHERE'S PENNY?"....................71
THE GREEN MAMBA 79
STRANGE LIGHT 85
THE CHARIOT OF THE PHARAOH 93
"IS THERE NO WAY OUT?"..............101
"THERE'S SOMEONE IN THIS ROOM!"......111
"THE WALL'S FALLING IN!".............117
SEPARATED 125
"WE'VE GOT THEM NOW!"...............131
"IT GOES STRAIGHT DOWN!"............139
"QUICK, PENNY! GET INSIDE!".........149
"THERE'S NO OTHER WAY!".............159
"THERE'S HOFFMANN!" 165
"TAKE OFF! TAKE OFF!"...............173
REST AT LAST 185

THE RAIDERS CONVERGE

The light plane swooped low over the jungle, swerving at times to avoid striking the clusters of taller trees that spiked up through the vegetation below. For a civilian plane, the craft was painted in a curious way—very much like a military aircraft, in fact. Dull green and dull khaki patches covered the tops and sides of the wings, tail, and body, while the bottom of the plane and its wings were painted in a lighter color. It was almost as if its owner didn't wanted the plane to be easily seen.

In fact, the owner of the aircraft did *not* want this craft to be easily seen! The man owned a number of planes, which he hired out for substantial fees. He didn't care if the aircraft were used for legal or illegal activities. In fact, he *knew* that many of those who rented them were operating far outside of the law. He cared only that the planes were returned intact, and that he was well paid for their use.

A shady character by the name of Stefan piloted this plane. He was a former member of the East German Secret Police. With the fall of the Soviet Union, some of these people had been placed in different units, under various names. They still worked for Moscow, and their aim was still to destabilize the Western Democracies. Under the revived totalitarian rule, Stefan had recently been assigned to Hoffmann's Africa team. Following orders, he had rented this plane for their mission, and scouted the area around the jungle camp where they would stay that night. He had also flown farther, and made one pass over the temple, which was their real destination.

Now he was flying Hoffmann to join the other members of the team.

The growing darkness was worrying Hoffmann, a lean, grim-faced, blond-haired man with fair complexion. Both he and the pilot beside him wore khaki shirts and trousers, both were soaked with sweat from the heat and humidity within the cockpit, and both were searching the terrain below. But Stefan was not worried; he knew where he was going and he knew how to get there. Hoffmann, on the other hand, had begun to fear that the sun's light would fail completely before they found the narrow landing strip in the darkness.

Suddenly Stefan unclipped his mike from the control panel and spoke into it. Instantly, a narrow landing strip in the jungle was illuminated by the headlights of the waiting Land Rover.

"There it is!" he said, as he dipped the nose of the craft for a moment so Hoffmann could see, and pointed at the sudden beams of light below.

"You can land *there*?" Hoffmann asked, incredulously, as the lights below were turned off.

"Of course," Stefan replied. "You'll see. It's wide enough and long enough, and it's fairly smooth. It was once a narrow road. I landed there last week and the ground is surprisingly even."

"And you're sure no one saw you?" Hoffmann asked quickly. "No one suspects that there's any activity at the end of that old road?"

"Very sure. I flew low the whole flight, scanned the horizon often, came to this camp by a very indirect course—just like today—and landed late in the afternoon. First I made a lazy circle before landing, to see that the sky was clear. That's how I scouted the temple, in fact, and made certain there was no one around to see me."

"We're cutting it close tonight," Hoffmann said. "The light's fading fast. You're sure you can do this?"

"Quite sure." The pilot was growing increasingly irritated by Hoffmann's questions. "Look," he said, finally, "you've got to trust me. I know my business." He was a large, powerfully muscled man, and he turned and frowned at his companion.

Hoffmann saw Stefan's irritation in the faint reflection of light from the instrument panel. He realized that there was no reason to antagonize a man whose services he needed.

"I do trust you, Stefan," he said firmly. "We've served together in Western Europe. But, you have to remember

I'm not a pilot. Flying low over jungles, like we're doing, and landing in narrow paths, like the one below, is not the way I usually travel." He smiled faintly.

Stefan accepted the apology and then gave his attention to the landing. Deliberately flying past the narrow strip, he turned the plane, and came in low and sure. Picking up his mike again, he spoke into it: "I'm coming in."

At once, the narrow road below was again outlined in the beams of the Land Rover.

The trees flashed by them as they swooped lower. Deftly, the pilot brought the craft to the ground. The light plane bounced along the narrow strip, slowing as it did so, closing rapidly toward the tall jungle at the end of the field. Hoffmann's fears as he saw this wall of trees and thick vegetation move swiftly toward them lasted only a few moments. The plane slowed almost to a stop; then the pilot made a sharp turn—at the very edge of the trees—and cut the engine. The Land Rover's headlights behind them went off at once.

"Good landing," Hoffmann said briefly, breathing a deep sigh of relief. He hadn't realized that he'd been holding his breath. "We'll spend the night here, with the men, then fly to the temple in the morning and take out all the treasure we can carry. It may take us two or three trips. We can't risk being discovered; we'll just have to bring out all we can each trip, and leave the rest. This raid will bring in millions for our cause."

"Kala does not know why we want this treasure, does he?" Stefan asked.

"No," Hoffmann replied, "just you and I and Walther. Kala thinks we're thieves like himself. He's with us because I've promised him we'll make a lot of money selling the temple treasures on the black market in Cairo. And I'll keep that promise—he will be paid. And we may use him again. But he has no idea that we're robbing this temple not just to make ourselves rich, but also for the cause of international socialism. He wouldn't understand that."

Not many people do," Stefan said, as he busied himself turning off the engine and the plane's instruments. "They live for themselves, not thinking of the poverty and misery of others. They have no idea that the injustices of the world will be ended when powerful centralized governments—like Russia's—rule the nations and administer the earth's resources for the benefit of all."

Hoffmann did not reply. He wondered if Stefan really believed the propaganda they each were spouting. Hoffmann himself no longer did. He knew the Russian rulers he served used Marxist theories to hoodwink their citizens into accepting totalitarian government. Hoffmann also knew he and Walther would be well paid. Stefan would get something for his work but he was on a lower level than Hoffmann and Walther, and wouldn't enjoy as much profit as they.

Their object was not only personal gain; it was also to secure the treasure so their espionage organization could step-up its activities against the western nations.

RETURN TO AFRICA

The sleek corporate jet touched down in the early afternoon, taxied to the hanger Jim Daring leased for his mining company's aircraft, and came to a halt. In a few moments, Mrs. Daring and four excited teenagers emerged from the plane and stepped down the ladder to the ground.

"Boy, is it good to be back in Africa!" Mark Daring exclaimed, breathing deeply as he looked around the busy airport. Mark was a powerfully built young man of seventeen, with blond hair and blue eyes, wearing khaki trousers and a blue polo shirt. "We've been away almost the whole summer!"

"We sure have," his sister Penny agreed. She was a slender girl, a year younger than Mark, with light brown hair and brown eyes. She couldn't wait to show her new friend, Maria, all the sights around her home in East Africa.

Maria was Penny's age, and at five feet seven, the same height as Penny. Her mother was a good friend of Mrs. Daring, and on their visit to Madrid, Spain, the Daring's had asked Maria to visit them in East Africa. This was

Maria's first visit to the continent, and her sparkling dark eyes showed that she was as excited to visit as Penny was to be home. Both girls wore casual skirts with light blouses.

"Well, I'm glad to be back," David Curtis agreed, "because you made a promise, Mark, and I'm holding you to it. You told me weeks ago that we'd explore an old temple your father's men had just discovered in the jungle."

David was seventeen, like Mark, but at six feet one he was two inches taller than his friend. And while Mark was stocky and solidly built, David was lean and slender, with dark hair and brown eyes. To Mark's continual astonishment, although David was not as thickly built, he was just as strong as Mark. The boys were great friends and competed with each other constantly. David wore khaki trousers, too, and a white polo shirt.

"Goodness, can't you people just enjoy the thought of *relaxing* for a few days?" Mrs. Daring asked with a smile. "After all the excitement you've had this summer, I'd think you'd be happy at the thought of coming home and just being *still!*"

Carolyn Daring was Mark's and Penny's mom. She'd been the one to interest her children in learning French, which had stood them in such good stead when they'd visited France for several weeks earlier that summer. But she had been appalled at the continual adventures that the teenagers had experienced, and she was very anxious for them to come home where they'd be *safe* as she put it.

She had flown back with the teenagers while her husband remained for several more days in Europe on business.

"Aw, Mom," Mark replied, "I told you that there's no danger in that temple. Mr. Rush scouted it from the air. Besides, we will relax for a couple of days. In fact, after all the danger David's gotten Penny and me into this summer, I insist that we take a break so we can restore our shattered nerves!"

"Mark," Maria laughed, "I don't see many signs of your shattered nerves. Do you, Mrs. Daring?"

"No, I don't, Maria," Mrs. Daring replied. "That's just a put-on. He doesn't mean it. But I mean it, young man!" she said emphatically, looking directly at her son. "You people are going to spend a few relaxing days around home before you go traipsing into the jungle to explore an old temple! Your father will finish his business in Madrid, then he'll come back. But until he returns, you're not budging from home! Goodness knows, with a swimming pool to enjoy, and everything else, you'll surely be happy spending some time right here!"

"We sure will, Mrs. Daring," David said hastily, wishing now that he hadn't mentioned exploring that ancient temple so soon. He sure didn't want to seem ungrateful to be a guest again in their home.

"We will, indeed, Mom," Mark assured her, giving her a hug with his strong arm. "And that'll give Maria a chance to get accustomed to Africa, and enjoy some of the things we were enjoying before David blew in from the States and turned our lives upside down!"

"Wait a minute," David protested. "I came for a quiet vacation. You and Penny are the ones who shoved me into troubles all summer. But don't worry, Mrs. Daring, I'll keep a brake on them for a while, and make sure they don't get Maria in any danger."

David winked at Mark as he said this, and Mark grinned back.

Just then one of the mechanics walked over from the waiting Cessna to help them get their bags from the corporate jet in which they'd arrived. Soon they'd transferred these to the smaller plane, one of the crafts belonging to Mr. Daring's mining company. They all got in, took their seats, and the pilot began the process of preparing for takeoff.

Ten minutes later they were in the air, heading upcountry for the Daring's home and mining company headquarters. David thought back to his first flight in this Cessna, when he'd flown in from the States almost three months before. He had a sudden thought.

With a wink at Mark to show he was teasing Penny, David asked, "None of you saw Hoffmann at the airport, did you?" He had to speak loudly because of the engine's noise.

Penny, seated ahead of him and across the aisle, looked back sharply. "David, that is not funny! Hoffmann is not something to joke about!" She clearly was not pleased.

"Aw, I was just remembering when I landed here at the beginning of the summer, and your Dad pointed out Hoffmann to us as we got in the car. We've got nothing to fear from him now. I was just joking."

"David's right," Mark said emphatically. "That man's out of our lives for good! Don't you remember the last time we ran into him, Penny? He was being chased by the German Army."

"Yes," she added, "and I also remember that they didn't catch him, either! No one seems able to catch him."

"Well, they probably have by now," Mark replied. "That man's history."

Hoffmann had been their deadly adversary throughout the summer. A former member of the STASI—the dreaded East German Secret Police under the Soviet rule—he had masterminded half a dozen illegal schemes to raise money for the very active Russian secret police. Mark, Penny, and David had somehow gotten mixed up with this dangerous foe all summer: in East Africa, Egypt, France, and Germany. The man seemed to turn up everywhere Mr. Daring had taken them on his business trips. The three teens had also managed to foil every one of his elaborate schemes, and for this they knew that they'd earned his undying hatred.

Now, however, Mark and David were sure that Hoffmann was out of their lives for good. But Penny had the strangest premonition that they had not seen the last of the deadly espionage agent. She shuddered, but said no more.

Two hours later, the aircraft swept in for a landing at the small field beside the headquarters of Jim Daring's mining company. David glanced out the window as they came in, and saw a dozen houses under the trees, several other structures, a radio tower, and a hanger.

In a short while the teenagers were in the pool, splashing and playing with ten-year-old Ruth, and seven-year-old Benjamin. The younger Daring children had sorely missed their brother and sister and David the previous weeks, and were delighted to have them back.

The exercise in the pool was a great relaxing way to end a day spent flying for hours in the confined seats of an airplane, and at dinner that evening the teenagers were in great spirits. After helping Mrs. Daring clean up from dinner, they played games with Ruth and Benjamin. Then Mrs. Daring and Penny put the young ones to bed.

When Penny rejoined Maria, she invited her to go with her to the room they used as a study and office. In addition to the radio, Maria noticed two desktop computers and a number of filing cabinets, while bookcases lined the other walls.

"Sit here, Maria," Penny said, pulling out a chair for her friend, beside the one she would use. "I've got to call Ellen Hawkins."

"And who is Ellen Hawkins?" Maria asked, sitting down and marveling at Penny's deft handling of the radio and its controls. *Penny can do so many things, she thought to herself.*

"She's a great friend," Penny replied. "Her father's a doctor, and they're at the Lutheran medical clinic upcountry. Ellen handles the office computers and keeps the records for her dad."

"And she plays chess with me by radio," Mark added, as he and David came into the room. "Tell her I said 'Hi'. And tell her I bought a chess book in Paris, and learned the French Defence, and intend to wipe her out in our next game."

Penny laughed. "Mark and Dad think Ellen's rather special because she loves to play chess, and she's good at it," she explained to Maria. "Personally, that game bores me to tears but the men find it fascinating." Soon Penny was in animated conversation with her friend on the radio. She introduced Maria and the Spanish girl spoke with Ellen for a few moments, before turning the call back to Penny.

Maria walked back into the living room and sat down with Mrs. Daring and the boys. "I've never spoken on shortwave before," she exclaimed.

"It's a lifesaver for us here," Mrs. Daring said. "We can keep in touch with people all over the country where the phone companies haven't yet moved in. But soon, I hope, they'll all have cellular connections, and that'll make things simpler for us."

"We'll get back to our weightlifting tomorrow morning! Boy, we've really been interrupted this summer," Mark said to David.

"That's the truth," David agreed. "And we'd better get back to sparring as well. We haven't sparred or wrestled for a long time. You've probably forgotten everything I taught you!"

"You taught me," Mark snorted." What a joke. I'll show you tomorrow how much I've remembered!"

"Mark," Mrs. Daring said, "I think Maria would be interested in looking through your telescope tomorrow night."

"We can turn out the lights around our house here," she explained to Maria, "and get a wonderful view of the heavens. And Mark's telescope shows us even more."

"You all have so many interests, Mrs. Daring," Maria said.

Carolyn Daring smiled at their new friend.

"Well, there are so many things to learn and do in this wide world that Jim and I determined we would keep our children from squandering their brains and their lives on video games and television like our friends back home," she replied with a smile. "So we've helped them pursue a number of hobbies, learn a lot about the world, learn to read and speak French—it's made life much more interesting for them. David's family did the same with their children."

"Well, you have certainly raised interesting children, Mrs. Daring. And I'm so delighted you invited me to visit your home. I love Madrid, it's my home, of course, but it's such a big city and it's so busy and everyone seems to be in such a hurry. But here, things are so peaceful."

Penny glanced suddenly at Mark, but he was looking at Maria and didn't notice the strange expression on his sister's face. Penny was thinking that things were peaceful now, but would they stay that way?

Penny kept her thoughts to herself.

TO THE TEMPLE

Four days later, the teens downed an early breakfast and piled into the van with their packs. Mr. Daring—who'd just returned from Madrid the day before—drove them to the hanger, where they found the smaller Cessna waiting for them. Daring pulled the van to a stop and they all got out and carried their packs to the plane.

"She's all set, Jim," the mechanic called, waving from the door of the hanger. "I've checked everything."

"Thanks, Ben," Jim Daring replied. He opened the plane's door and climbed in, then turned and took the packs David and Mark handed him and stowed these behind the back seats. Then he got out, and while Penny and Maria walked over to speak to Ben, he and Mark and David walked around the plane, checking everything. When they'd completed their inspection, Jim Daring stopped and grinned at the boys.

"Looks like you're all set to go," he said. "Wish I could go with you."

"C'mon, Dad," Mark replied at once. "You know we want you along!"

"Thanks, Mark, but I made the mistake of stopping at the office when I got in last night and saw the mountain of paper on my desk. I've got to tackle that stuff right away. If the temple is really interesting, maybe we can all go back there next week."

"We'll check it out for you, Mr. Daring," David said. He knew he'd want to go back again.

Daring turned to the preparations at hand. "Got all your stuff? Food, water, lights, pistols?"

"Yes, sir," Mark replied. "We've got our food, we've each got canteens in our daypacks, there's extra water in the plane, and we've all got flashlights. We're ready."

"And you've got the revolvers?"

"Yes, sir," Mark replied. "We've got those in that small gray pack—guns, holsters, ammo."

The Darings always carried powerful revolvers when they flew over the jungle, just in case they ran into packs of wild pigs or wild dogs. They also took food and emergency supplies with them when they flew—people in the past had perished when their planes went down and they had not prepared themselves to survive before rescue arrived.

"And the rope you suggested, sir," David added. "We've brought that along."

"Good," Jim Daring said approvingly. "I doubt you'll need it, but you never can tell."

The boys wore sheath knives in case they needed to cut away branches to get into the temple. Both they and the girls wore sturdy khaki pants, long-sleeved shirts, and tough hiking shoes. The girls had brought their cameras. Seeing that the men were ready, Penny and Maria walked over and joined them.

"Let's pray for a safe trip," Jim Daring said. The four teenagers gathered around him as he asked the Lord to give them safety in travel, as well as in their exploration of the temple.

Then Jim Daring hugged the girls, shook Mark's and David's hands, and walked back to the hanger door. Penny and Maria climbed into the plane and went to the back seats of the four-passenger craft. Mark got in the pilot's place and David sat beside him. When they'd buckled up, Mark began the procedure for take-off. David glanced at his watch; it was seven o'clock in the morning. Mark started the engine and the plane began to move as he taxied to the runway. They all waved to Jim Daring and the mechanic.

A few moments later they were in the air, climbing for altitude. Maria peered through the window at the mining station below.

"Look how small the houses seem already," she exclaimed.

"And the people," Penny added. "There's Ruth and Benjamin waving from the front of our home, but they look tiny from here!"

Mark circled the group of houses where the families lived, and waggled the plane's wings in response to the children below. Then he turned the plane in a graceful curve and settled on a course for the mountains.

"I've wanted to head for those mountains since the day I first came here," David said to Mark.

"So have I," Mark replied. They had to speak loudly above the noise of the plane's engine. "And I've been to parts of them, over to the right, where there's a large lake. But I haven't seen this temple yet."

"How did your dad's men find it?" David asked, intrigued.

"They were doing an aerial survey and when they flew low, they saw in a clearing a huge mound covered with vegetation. They'd wondered about it before, but this time they were looking at it from a lower altitude. There'd been a big storm the week before, and apparently the winds had torn away some of the jungle vegetation. Now they could see part of a stone building they hadn't ever seen. No one had suspected it was there. And they don't know of any records about it. It's a real mystery!"

"Sure it's legal for us to go inside?" David asked.

"Yep. Dad checked with Colonel Lamumba at army headquarters. He's in charge of this district. And he said we could. Dad's firm has done a lot for the government, and he and Colonel Lamumba are good friends."

"And even your mom is satisfied that it's safe for us to make this trip?" David asked in wonder.

"Even Mom," Mark replied. "Colonel Lamumba took a helicopter and looked it over. He landed beside it, he told Dad, scouted part of the grounds, and even went inside. He saw some of the rooms and said it looked harmless enough, and told Dad we could explore it if we wanted to. We just have to keep an eye out for snakes, of course."

"Well, we do that in Alabama," David said. "We've got some deadly ones there: copperheads, coral snakes, moccasins."

"Sure, and we've got some bad ones here, too," Mark replied.

The countryside they were flying over was covered with tall trees that effectively hid the jungle floor beneath. David wondered what the ground was like under those branches. Then he saw a familiar sight, and pointed it out to Mark.

"That's the river we flew over on the way to Colonel Lamumba's headquarters when we identified those men who'd kidnapped Mr. Rush," he said.

"That's it," Mark agreed. "And over there is the river where we fought those crocodiles. Man, seems like that was years ago!"

"It sure does," David agreed. "But they never did get all of Hoffmann's gang, did they?"

"No," Mark replied, "they didn't. Some of them escaped. And in fact—" he said in a lower tone, leaning toward David so the girls behind him wouldn't hear as he spoke above the engine's noise, "—the big German named

Walther got away later, Dad told me. So did the African knife-fighter named Kala.

David's face showed his surprise. "Walther? He was Hoffmann's lieutenant from the East German Secret Police, wasn't he?"

"That's right," Mark answered. "They captured him after we escaped from the crocodiles, but a few weeks ago he got away somehow, and then just disappeared."

"Wonder how many of Hoffmann's men are still in the country?" David asked.

"Well, a few, but they're scattered, the Colonel told Dad. And since they're scattered, they're not organized. Colonel Lamumba assured Dad that they don't pose a threat to the mining companies anymore."

"Do Hoffmann's men know about this temple where we're going?" David asked suddenly.

"Don't see how they could," Mark replied. "Colonel Lamumba said his pilot was sworn to secrecy about the place."

"But could Sanderson have told Hoffmann about it? Remember, he'd been spying in your dad's office, and tipped Hoffmann off about the buried tomb."

Mark's friendly face clouded as he thought about this. "You're right. But I don't remember dad mentioning anything about Hoffmann learning of this temple."

Both boys looked somber as they pondered the thought of Hoffmann and his gang. Then David said, "Well, the Colonel is convinced that wherever he may be,

Hoffmann's not in this part of the country. He's confident enough to let us visit the temple. I think we've got nothing to worry about."

"I agree," Mark replied.

David glanced back suddenly, to make sure the girls had not overheard this conversation. He saw at once that they were busy talking amongst themselves. The plane's engine made such a noise they couldn't have understood the boys' words anyway. Reassured, David relaxed.

Behind the two boys, Penny and Maria were looking out the windows, taking turns looking through Penny's single lens reflex camera with a telephoto lens. "It's just like having powerful binoculars," Penny leaned across the aisle and told her friend. "But I'll use the wide-angle lens in the temple. We should get some fine pictures there."

Shortly after nine, they were flying over the foothills of the long mountain range. Mark pointed over to the right; the others looked, and saw the large lake in the distance. "That's a beautiful spot we've never explored," he said. "We've got to go there next."

Then Mark turned left, and began to follow the course of a long valley. He pushed the wheel forward, reduced speed, and the Cessna began to descend. Soon the mountain peaks towered above them to the right. A small river, or large stream, appeared and disappeared through the trees below.

"I'm following that stream," Mark told David. "That'll lead us. We're looking for the stream to make a right-angle jog. The valley widens there, and gives us room to land beside the temple."

Ten minutes later David spotted it. "That's it, Mark."

Ahead of them, the valley had widened. The stream made a sharp turn before heading back on its original course, and then disappeared under a steep mound.

"That's the spot where the temple should be," Mark said. "It looks like a hill, but the temples underneath that vegetation, the Colonel said. The stream seems to go underground as it heads to the temple's mound from the north; then it emerges at the south end and continues toward the jungle."

"There's the level place for our landing," David said. And then he pointed excitedly, "And look! There's a small patch of the temple showing through the vegetation that covers the temple!"

"That's it," Mark said. He turned back to the girls. "We've found it." Then he swept the plane in a tight turn over the jungle, searching carefully, studying the narrow level place where the Colonel had told him he could land.

"Looks okay to me," he said to David. "What do you think?"

"Looks good to me, too," David replied.

Then Mark pointed in surprise: "Look! There's another level strip of ground on the other side of the temple. Which place would you pick to land?"

"This near one," David said at once. "The Colonel didn't mention one on the far side of the temple. I'd stick with this one."

Mark flew low over the narrow level spot between the mound and the trees, studying the ground carefully, making sure it was safe to land. Then he turned back, swept around the temple again, and headed for the ground. "Hold on," he called back to Penny and Maria. "We're landing."

"This is the most exciting part for me," Penny said to Maria, eyes shining. "I love to land."

Then the Cessna touched down between the vine-covered temple and the jungle. Mark was exceedingly careful, but the ground was remarkably level and the landing was smooth. He taxied toward the hill, swung the plane around under the branches of the tall trees, and cut the engine.

"That was a great landing, Mark!" Penny exclaimed.

"Thanks," he grinned. "The ground's better than I expected. Let's look around first before we get out."

Penny saw the puzzled expression on Maria's face at Mark's words, so she explained. "We always look around in a strange place," she said to her Spanish friend. "There may be wild dogs or wild pigs. You never know."

For several minutes, the four teens peered through the windows of the plane, scanning the jungle. But nothing ominous appeared, so Mark said finally, "Let's go."

David opened the door and got out, Mark followed, and then the girls. The four stretched for a minute and looked around.

"I can just see part of the temple through that torn vegetation!" Maria said, pointing to a spot in the sloping side of the mound, through which they could see dark stone. "Isn't this exciting?"

"The clearing is so peaceful," Penny said, smiling at David, who grinned back.

"Just what we ordered for you girls," he replied.

TRAPPED

"This is fantastic!" Maria exclaimed, ecstatic. "Imagine we're about to explore an ancient temple. My friends in Madrid would never believe this."

"Neither would mine in Montgomery," David agreed. "This whole summer has been fantastic."

"And we've even got a breeze to blow away the heat," Mark added.

"Oh, it's so mysterious," Penny said, pointing toward the steep green mound of vegetation under which the ancient temple was concealed. "Imagine. This temple has been buried under all that stuff for centuries maybe, and no one's known about it until now."

"That's why I just can't believe this is happening to me," Maria exclaimed. "Never in my wildest dreams did I think I'd be doing something like this!"

"Let's get our gear together," Mark said, as he climbed back into the aircraft, and began handing their packs to David. Mark shoved the small gray pack with the pistols forward, out of the way while he handled the others—and David failed to notice this.

The gray pack remained in the plane.

Mark then emerged with the cooler and a package of plastic cups. They took the opportunity to drink some lemonade, and at Mark's suggestion dug into some of their snacks.

"It's good to stand for a while," David said, stretching. "I got cramped just sitting in the plane."

"We'll get some good exercise climbing around in there and exploring," Mark said with anticipation.

"Do you really think you'll need that rope?" Penny asked David, as she saw him stuff the coil into his daypack.

"Probably not," he replied with a grin. "But your dad thought it was a good idea to take it along. Better to have it and not need it, than need it and not have it." David couldn't keep the excitement out of his voice and Penny smiled at his enthusiasm.

"Got your camera?" Penny asked Maria.

"Yes," Maria said, pulling this out of her pack and hanging it by its strap around her shoulder.

"Zip those packs closed," Mark advised the girls. "You don't want spiders crawling in."

Hastily, Penny and Maria checked their packs to make sure that they were securely closed. Then they all strapped on their small daypacks.

"Well, let's go," David said. "Time's flying."

The boys had made a curious and uncharacteristic mistake. Each thought that the other had brought the small gray pack that held the pistols in their belted holsters. Ordinarily, they strapped on the revolvers when they left the aircraft. This time they did not.

The four began to walk toward the hill that rose before them. The birds had been silenced by the noise of the plane when it landed, but now they had begun to sing again.

"Look at the flowers," Penny said, pointing to a riot of red flowers interspersed in the thick vines and leaves that covered the stone temple.

As they got closer, Penny took out her camera. "I haven't seen this kind before," she said, changing lenses as she approached the brilliant wild flowers. "They're beautiful!"

"Well, I know a lot of the flowers in Spain," Maria said with a laugh, "but these are all new to me." Maria's English was flawless, but her accent intrigued her friends, and they loved to hear her speak.

They came close to the steeply rising temple mound and stopped. As Penny began to frame careful shots of the flowers, Mark spoke quietly to Maria: "Penny's a good photographer. You should see the pictures she's got back at the house."

"I saw some of them," Maria replied. "The ones she'd framed on her wall. How did she learn to take such pictures?"

"From Mom. Mom's great, and she taught Penny. She'll get some fine pictures of these."

David began to walk to the left, looking more closely at the wall of green before them, heading toward the tear in the vegetation through which they had seen the stone wall of the temple. In a minute, he found it, about thirty feet above the ground. A patch of leaf-covered vine had been ripped away by the wind, and was hanging down. And then David saw the tunnel opening that Colonel Lamumba had spoken of, the opening that led into the temple itself. He looked closely at the hanging vine. *That makes a handy ladder!* he thought. To reach the tunnel opening he'd have to climb up the steep vine-covered slope, and he realized he could use the vine for his climb.

"Wonder what kind of stone this is?" he asked aloud, of no one in particular. Grabbing the hanging vine, David put his feet in the thickly matted vegetation that covered the temple, and began to climb. It was surprisingly easy, and he made rapid progress. He had no trouble finding footholds in the vines as he climbed upward, and soon he had reached a ledge that projected from the temple wall. Climbing over this, he stepped onto the narrow stone ledge. He braced his feet firmly on this, then pulled the hanging vines to the side and exposed more of the wall and the narrow door-shaped opening that led inside.

The stone was black, smooth, cold. He looked up to see the size of the blocks, but couldn't find a seam. *Boy, these must be big blocks of stone*, he thought. Then he began to wonder who had built the structure, and when they had done it.

FLIGHT FROM THE TEMPLE

A strange sense of timelessness engulfed him, almost as if he'd gone back into the past, to the time when the temple had been constructed. *Wonder what kind of gods they worshipped here?* he thought, with a slight shiver.

David pulled his flashlight from its case on his belt, turned it on, and flashed this into the opening of the tunnel. The ceiling was about eight feet high, he guessed. The passage was maybe four feet wide, but he couldn't see where it ended. The powerful beam just became lost in the darkness ahead. Then he heard Mark's voice behind and below him.

"Hey, wait for us!" David turned, and saw his friends hurrying over to join him.

"Watch your step," he said, "it's steep. But there are good places for your feet in the vines. Just go slow and use the hanging vine as a rope to pull on. It's easy."

Penny climbed up first, then Maria. David helped each of them over the ledge, and moved into the entrance of the tunnel to give them room to stand. Then Mark climbed up and joined them.

David stepped into the tunnel, and Penny and Maria followed him. Mark remained on the ledge, just outside the opening.

"What do you see in there?" he asked.

"Nothing," David replied. "Just a tunnel. Ready to explore?"

"Boy, I'll say we are," Mark agreed. "Let's go." Then Mark remembered something else. As David walked away into the temple, Mark asked: "Did you bring that bag with the pistols?"

"No," David replied. He stopped and looked back at Mark.

"I'll get it," Mark said at once. "You all go ahead."

"Everybody get out your flashlights," David advised, as he began to follow the strong beam of his light into the darkness. Penny came next, then Maria.

"We won't go far," David called back to Mark.

Mark stepped back to the ledge and glanced at the plane parked thirty yards away. He was about to climb down to the ground when he saw something that made his heart skip a beat: half-a-dozen wild pigs had trotted rapidly out of the jungle behind the Cessna, and were heading directly toward the temple.

His heart froze! *How'll I get back to the plane with those beasts there?* he wondered.

Suddenly one of the dark-skinned pigs snorted wildly, circled with his snout to the ground, and then dashed toward the temple, right along the path the teenagers had taken! The others dashed after him and they all came to a sudden stop at the bottom of the vine-covered stone wall. Here they began to circle rapidly about, grunting with anger as they all picked up the scent of the teenagers' path. Their sharp tusks gleamed in the sunlight.

They've found our scent! Mark thought, his heart pounding. Quickly he turned toward the others, and started to speak. But they had already moved some distance into the dark tunnel, following the beams of their lights.

Now Mark wondered what to do. Should he tell them about the deadly wild pigs, or wait until later? He wrestled with this for a moment. Then he decided to wait. *No sense scaring them now!* he thought. *Those animals sure can't climb up here. And maybe they'll be gone when we get back; Colonel Lamumba didn't mention them, so maybe they're just passing by.*

With a strange premonition that the four of them were moving into great danger, Mark turned on his flashlight and hurried to catch up with the others. His mind was in turmoil. *If those wild pigs don't leave, we won't be able to get back to the plane! We'll be trapped in the temple!*

"WATCH FOR SNAKES!"

The small plane swooped low over the jungle, dipping into valleys wherever possible, as Stefan made every move he could to keep the craft from being spotted.

"Maybe I'm getting used to flying this low," Hoffmann had said once, with a faint, a very faint, smile. He wasn't going to criticize Stefan again, but brushing the treetops sure made him nervous. Hoffmann's eyes were cold like steel, Stefan thought. His face, especially his nose, showed signs of recent damage.

"No worry," Stefan replied. "I just want to make sure no one sees us."

"But you said this part of the country is uninhabited."

"It is," Stefan responded. "But there's always the occasional hunter or explorer. I've scouted this place twice this week, and there's been no report that I've been noticed. And our spy in the district army headquarters assured me that no one knows what I've been doing. I mean to keep it that way."

Hoffmann didn't argue. This man knew his business. Hoffmann knew he was a fine pilot. *I've got to trust him, he thought.*

"You're sure there's treasure in this temple?" Hoffmann asked.

"You bet I'm sure," Stefan replied. "Jim Daring's mining engineer, Tom Rush, found the place. Then Colonel Lamumba went to scout it for them. Daring does a lot of work for the government, you know. Our man in Lamumba's office said that the Colonel told Daring over the radio there was nothing valuable in the old place. But later Lamumba radioed him and said he could send a plane up there! Obviously, in the first message he was trying to fool anyone listening into thinking there was nothing worth looking for."

Stefan swerved the plane suddenly, swooping around a cluster of tall trees that seemed to leap up from the jungle below. Then he brought the craft back on course, and continued his explanation to Hoffmann.

"Now, why would Daring send a plane to the temple if there wasn't something there? Daring's a mining engineer. He finds diamond fields and valuable mineral deposits. You *know* he's found something and the government's covering for him while he explores it."

"Makes sense to me," Hoffmann replied. His face twisted into a bitter smile. "It's time I got back at Daring," he snarled. "That man and his kids have foiled me half-a-dozen times this summer. Robbed us of millions we could have used to finance our espionage in Western Europe. He's got two teenage kids, and they've got a friend visiting them from America. You don't know what those people have done to us. They've made us lose fortunes. And a lot of good men have been captured and jailed because of them and their luck. Just when we're about to make a killing, those kids have gotten in our way and called the army or police in on us."

He clenched his teeth and pounded his fist on the panel in front of him. "We've got a score to settle with Daring, all right. This will be a pleasure, getting to this treasure before he does."

Behind Hoffmann, the big German, Walther, and the small but deadly African knife fighter named Kala, slouched in the cramped seats. Their gear filled the compartment behind them. The two had been captured by Colonel Lamumba's men at the beginning of the summer, after trying to capture Penny Daring to hold for ransom. But Hoffmann had paid for men to break them out of Lamumba's jail, and they were once again part of his gang in this raid on the temple. "We'll make a fortune personally," he promised them.

"What's your plan?" the pilot asked Hoffmann

"We'll go through that opening your man said Colonel Lamumba found, then explore the place as quickly as we can. We've got high-tech instruments; you wouldn't believe what these can tell us. It won't take us long to scout the place and find the treasure. And we've got explosives.

Walther is an expert with that stuff. Our instruments can find hidden rooms, and he can blow holes in the walls and get us in."

"Can he blow holes in the walls without bringing the whole place down on our heads?" Stefan asked. He hated the thought of crawling into a huge stone temple. He liked the sky, and lots of room, and the prospect of crawling around inside a stone temple did not appeal to him at all.

"He can blow holes in the wall beside you, and you wouldn't know he'd done it," Hoffmann assured him, exaggerating for emphasis. "The man's a genius with explosives. By the way, will you need to scout the landing before you land?"

"No. I'm staying low, remember. Besides, I've found it from the air. I'll fly straight into that narrow strip this side of the temple hill and land on the first pass. Then we'll hide the plane under the tall trees, just in case someone flies over while we're on the ground."

The plane swept low toward the level strip of ground between the temple mound and the trees, and coasted in for a landing. The mound was between them and the Cessna the teenagers had used, and Hoffmann and his men never even saw the other plane.

Stefan made a smooth landing, turned the aircraft toward the nearby trees, and killed the engine. The four men got out at once and pulled the plane deeper into the cover of the tall branches overhead, turning it around to be ready for a quick take-off when they returned. Rapidly they unloaded their gear, setting the packs carefully on the ground.

"Shall we bring the AK-47s?" Walther asked, pointing to the bag that held the automatic weapons.

"No," Hoffmann replied. "We can't shoot inside that temple; we'd blow out our ear drums. Leave them in the plane."

"But you said Walther could use explosives if we needed to," Stefan protested, surprised.

"Walther can use explosives," Hoffmann retorted, "not us. He's a genius with them. But he uses small amounts and positions them so they won't create sound waves to disturb that temple or wreck our ears. But our guns take no such precautions, and we can't risk shooting inside. Leave 'em here."

Walther put the bag with the automatic rifles back into the aircraft, and the four men picked up their packs and headed toward the temple. Hoffmann and the pilot led, Walther and Kala followed.

"Where's the opening?" Hoffmann asked, as they approached the steep side of the temple mound.

"There's a couple of them, in fact, one on the other side, but we're looking for one that's about a dozen feet above the ground," Stefan replied. "The infrared pictures my photographer took showed an opening right over there." He pointed above them, as he led the men to the base of the mound.

"Wait here," he said, setting down his pack. "I'll find it." Grabbing the thick vines, he began to work his way up the side of the temple. The others watched him as he ascended.

"We'll have to use rope to lower the stuff we bring out," Walther commented quietly.

"We've got plenty of that," Hoffmann assured him.

Kala said nothing. He was asking himself—not for the first, nor for the last time—why he'd agreed to work with these men again. He'd been arrested and jailed at the beginning of the summer, and it had taken Hoffmann's men eight weeks to break him out. *Now, here I am, working for Hoffmann again*, he thought ruefully to himself. Then he thought of the money, and decided it was worth it.

Meanwhile, the pilot was scrambling up the thick netting of matted vine and vegetation. Finally he stopped. Whipping out his sheath knife, he began to cut strips in the vines.

"This is it," he called to the men below. "I'll cut out a panel in this green stuff, one we can open, then fold back when we leave. We don't want anything suspicious to be visible from the air." In a few minutes, the pilot had cut out a wider panel in the thick vegetation and vines. "Come on," he called. He slipped the long knife back in its sheath, and pulled his big flashlight from its loop in his belt. "I'll look inside."

"I'll go up and toss you this line," Hoffmann told the other men, picking up the coil of rope Walther had thrown on the ground. Hoffmann scrambled up the vines and reached the place where the pilot had enlarged the opening. Then he tossed one end of the rope to the men below. One at a time, the four bags of gear were tied to the rope and hauled up the steep side of the mound. Stefan came back to the entrance of the passage just as Kala and Walther had climbed up and joined Hoffmann.

"Let's go," Hoffmann said crisply, shouldering one of the bags. The others picked up their bags and flashlights.

"Watch for snakes," Stefan warned, as he led them into the passage. "And hope that we don't run across any green mambas. One of those would kill the four of us before we could get away!"

"You're kidding," Hoffmann said in surprise. Walther laughed skeptically.

"I'm not kidding at all. Green mambas have actually attacked safaris and bitten half a dozen men before anyone could stop them. When one of those snakes bites you, you die at once. They're awful!"

"WHICH WAY?"

David came to a stop, and the others did too.

"Our first decision," he said, flashing his light to the left and to the right. The passage had come to a dead end, and then split to each side at right angles. Mark, Penny, and Maria crowded around him, shining their lights down the halls on each side. The beams cast eerie shadows on the walls, and Maria huddled closer to Penny.

"I'd say right," Mark said. "We flew in from the eastern side of the temple. And we got in the temple on that side, but near the south end. So the main part of the temple is to our right. "

"Makes sense to me," David said. He turned right, his flashlight piercing the darkness far down the passage, then closer on the ground in front of his feet as he walked. Penny came next, and she too flashed her light on the ground before her. Maria did the same. Mark was last.

"I can't tell what color this stone is," Penny said, her voice magnified strangely by the stone passage.

"I think it's a kind of dark green," Maria said, "But I'm not sure."

"It's mighty smooth," David commented, running his hand along the wall beside him. "Whoever cut these stones spent a lot of time smoothing and polishing them."

"This must have taken *years* to build," Maria said.

"Must have," Mark agreed. "I bet it's got several levels, and maybe some below the ground."

"I feel fresh air," Penny said suddenly.

The others did too. "That's good news," David exclaimed.

"That's what the Colonel said we'd find," Mark reminded them. "He said there was fresh air in the corridors they explored. Wonder where it comes from?"

"Here's the first room," David said suddenly, stepping out of the dark passage and flashing his light around him. The others crowded around, shining their lights to left and right. They saw that the room was square, perhaps fifty feet to a side.

"And there's one of the idols the colonel saw," Mark said, aiming the beam of his light at a tall grim figure in black stone that stood before them. Behind this, a double row of large stone blocks stretched back to the wall.

Slowly the four walked toward the stone idol and came to a stop before it.

"What is it?" Maria asked, shuddering slightly.

"It's one of their gods, I think," Penny replied. "Look at the animal's head on a man's body - it's a crocodile head."

FLIGHT FROM THE TEMPLE

The black stone idol was polished smooth. Its arms were crossed over the chest. Clenched fists gripped strange short rods with the heads of serpents facing outward. Mark stepped closer and flashed his light around the idol's torso. "Look at the marks on his body," he said.

The others clustered around and peered at the strange marks that seemed to encircle the idol's chest, sides, and back.

"I've seen those somewhere," Penny said suddenly.

"Where?" Mark asked sharply. He'd heard the slight shaking in her voice.

"I...I'm just not *sure*," she said again. She trembled. "Maybe..." she began, then stopped.

"Yes," Mark urged.

"Maybe it was when we went to that temple last year, Mark, where they used to sacrifice people to their gods. Remember?"

"Yeah," Mark said slowly, frowning. "I remember. That was an awful place."

"It was terrible," Penny said. She felt suddenly cold all over.

"Let's keep moving," David suggested quietly, stepping around the idol and aiming his beam down the lane between the rows of stone blocks that towered above their heads. "There's the door that leads out of here."

The others followed him around the idol, past the blocks, and toward the door. "I hope we don't see any more of those," Penny said, as they walked again in single file through the door. They were in a tunnel again.

"So do I," Maria agreed. She hadn't liked the look on the idol's animal face, or the look on Penny's face either. *Penny's scared!* Maria thought to herself. *Why would a stone idol make Penny scared like that?*

Troubled now, Maria walked rapidly behind Penny, who was following David. Mark came behind. Strangely, the four became silent. No one could think of anything to say. With quiet steps they walked through the passage, following the beams of their flashlights.

Mark's voice suddenly broke their silence. "The Colonel told Dad that he hadn't had time to go past that first room."

No one replied. They all realized that they were going where no one had gone - for centuries, maybe.

Then another room opened before them, and here they came to a halt. Twice as large as the first room they'd entered, the ceiling of this one was also much higher.

"Wow!" David said in awe, as he swept his light slowly around the wall to his right. "Look at those."

Five rows of tall warrior's shields hung on the wall. Between the tall shields were long-bladed spears, fixed to the wall. Their gold-covered blades gleamed as the beams of the flashlights swept over them.

Mark shone his light on the wall to their left. There also were rows of shields interspersed with long spears.

The walls seemed to be almost black in the light of their flashlights, yet highly polished, and they reflected back the beams from the lights as if they were mirrors.

"Wow," Mark said.

"Look ahead." David said. He swept his beam slowly from left to right, and they saw a row of stone statues before them. The figures were of men, very tall, very dark. Each man held by his side a spear, with the end on the ground and the point aimed toward the ceiling. "Those are warriors," David said quietly. Suddenly he was breathing rapidly, nervously. The others were too.

"There are twelve of them," Penny said in a small voice.

"They seem *alive*," Maria said.

For a moment no one moved. Then David spoke. "Well, they're just stone statues, nothing for us to be afraid of. Let's go closer." He stepped toward the rank of stone men, and the others walked with him.

But as they came closer, they all began to walk more slowly. Then, as if by common consent, the four came to a halt. They stood now just six feet away from the row of warriors. And the four felt small, insignificant, threatened by the fierce faces and long iron-tipped spears.

"They look like they're guarding something," Penny said, breaking the nervous silence.

"I bet they are," Mark replied. "I bet they're guarding that altar behind them."

David stepped several feet to his left, and shined his light between two of the tall warriors. "You're right," he replied. "And there's a larger door behind that altar. They're guarding that, too."

Maria shone her light on the wall to the left, then quickly to the right. "Look," she said, "there are more warriors standing against both walls! These are all guards, aren't they?" she asked.

"I think so," David answered.

"I bet they're to warn people not to go any farther," Penny said suddenly. She was trying hard to remember what she and Mark had heard about that temple they'd seen last year. She just *knew* there was something she should remember, something that mattered, that they should know, but she couldn't bring it to mind. She did remember that the Colonel had told them of the ancient commerce between this part of East Africa and Egypt, and the similar art and statuary found in the temples in each place.

David interrupted Penn's thoughts. "Let's go past that altar and through the door."

"Can we go around those men, instead of between them?" Maria asked. She too had a sense of great danger from the towering silent warriors.

"Sure," David said. He walked to his left, and the others walked with him, past the row of figures that stood guard with such silent and implacable menace. They made a wide circle past the altar the warriors were guarding—no one wanted to go close to that—and turned back toward the door set in the middle of the far wall.

This door was wider than the one through which they'd entered the room. And their beams revealed strange stone figures on either side of the doorway. These also were statues of warriors, they saw, standing on blocks that raised them several feet above the floor. The warriors were facing each other on either side of the doorway, their arms were raised above their heads, and their hands held up what appeared to be a great wheel made of stone. The teens stopped.

"What's that wheel they're holding?" Penny asked, puzzled.

"It's got strange marks and designs on it," Maria observed, sweeping her light slowly around the large stone.

"It looks like its got daggers sticking out all around it," David commented. "Wonder what that's supposed to mean?"

"Do you think it's a symbol that the warriors are guarding the door?" Penny asked. "Those daggers point everywhere. Maybe that means that they're ready to repel intruders from every direction."

"Maybe that's what it is," David answered. "But it's pretty high above the door. How could it guard the door if it's twelve feet above it?"

"Well, we could get pretty fanciful if we wanted to," Mark commented dryly, trying to break their increasingly fearful mood. "But I don't think we're going to be able to decipher all the symbols we see in this place. Let's just go on and see what we find."

Each of them felt mystified by the strange stone circle above the door. But they wanted to get out of that room. So they began to move slowly toward the door. David led, Penny and Maria walked side by side, and Mark came last.

"That's a different color," Penny commented, flashing her light on a rectangular block of stone in the floor on which they had to step to go through the door.

"And look at those strange designs," Maria said aiming her light at the weird and fierce-looking faces carved in the stone that glared up at them. David stepped on the block, the girls stepped right behind him, and a sharp crack split the air above them.

"Watch out," Mark cried, as he leaped forward, threw his arms around each girl's shoulders and propelled them through the door as the horrible sound of stone scraping on stone screamed down from directly above.

"WE CAN'T GO BACK!"

Their ears were stunned by the terrifying sound of disintegrating blocks of tumbling stone as the huge dagger-tipped wheel fell from the collapsed arms that held it and plunged toward the floor.

At Mark's yell, David had whirled around, reaching out for the girls as he stumbled backwards into the room and fell. Mark had propelled Penny and Maria into the room, and they had all fallen to the floor just inside the doorway. Shaken, a bit bruised, but unhurt, they scrambled to their feet and backed away from the smashing rock and rising dust.

"What happened?" Maria cried.

"That stone wheel the warriors were holding fell when you stepped on that different colored block!" Mark said. "Did I hurt you?" He'd landed hard on one knee as he'd shoved the girls forward and tried to break his fall so he wouldn't hit them with his heavy body. Now he stooped and rubbed a painful bruise.

"No," they both said at once.

"But you sure scared us," Penny said.

"When you three stepped on that block I heard a crack, and when I looked up the arms of those warriors were collapsing, and the big wheel with the daggers started to fall," Mark said. "That's why I leaped at you to push you out of the way!"

"It's a good thing you did!" David said in a shocked voice. "And you just made it through yourself! That stone on the floor must have had ropes inside the wall leading to the top of the door that triggered that trap!"

"Now I remember what it was about that temple we saw a year ago, Mark!" Penny said in a small voice.

"What was it?" he asked.

"The guide told us that the place had lots of deadly traps: at the doors, by the walls, in the ceilings. There were all kinds of traps to keep strangers out of the rooms, or kill them if they entered. And this temple has statues just like that one did."

"That's one of the traps, then," Mark said, shining his light on the doorway behind them. The others turned and flashed their lights back at the doorway and gasped at the sight of the large stone wheel blocking the door. No one said anything for a long moment. Then, finally, Penny broke the stunned silence. "Now we can't go back."

Mark was the first to reply. "I'm afraid you're right."

Then he thought of the wild pigs he'd seen outside the temple. *Those pigs won't let us get back to the plane, either.* Once more he wondered if he should mention this to the others. But again he decided to wait. *They've got enough to worry about now,* he thought.

"Well, we can't go that way, but there's got to be lots of other ways out of here." David said confidently. "After all, the temple's got four sides and four levels at least. There must be other doorways like the one we entered, and maybe even windows."

They all hoped he was right.

"We'd better keep going, then," Mark said quietly.

"And we'd better watch for more traps like that one," Penny warned, as she fell into step beside David.

This passage was wider and the four moved quickly behind the beams of their flashlights. In a few moments they came to a stairway which was as wide as the passage itself. This led upwards, they saw, and the four stopped before the first step and flashed their lights on the stones before their feet.

"See anything different?" David asked.

"Nope," Mark replied.

"Neither do I," Penny said. Maria nodded in silent agreement.

"Let me go first," Mark said suddenly, but David stepped ahead of him.

"I'll go," he said quickly. "You've already had a fall. Let me check it out."

Swiftly David walked up the steps, shining his light upward, then on the walls, then on the steps again, then ahead. But on neither the walls nor the steps did he notice any sign of anything sinister, or anything that might have signaled a trap.

"Be careful, David," Penny called, as he continued to ascend the steps.

"It's okay," he called back, as he reached the next level. "Come on up. There's another room."

"Go ahead, girls," Mark urged.

Penny and Maria ascended quickly, with Mark right behind. Soon the four were standing in front of another doorway, one not as tall as the one with the two warriors holding the stone wheel.

"See anything suspicious?" David asked.

None did. But they searched the walls and ceiling and floor carefully in the beams of their powerful flashlights. Nothing seemed different. Nothing appeared dangerous.

"This time I'll go ahead," Mark said firmly, as he brushed past David and entered the room. Quickly he flashed his light all around him, searching the walls, the ceiling, the floor, and the wall on the far side.

"Come on in," he said.

David followed Maria and Penny into the room. Here the four stood for a moment and looked around. The room was not large as the other had been, but it too had statues of warriors along the walls. There was also a cluster of statues in the middle of the room. These were smaller than the others they'd seen.

"These men don't have spears," Penny said suddenly.

"Wonder why not?" Mark asked, puzzled.

"I guess it's a different kind of room," David said. "Do they look like priests, or witch doctors?"

"I can't tell," Penny answered. "But maybe this room doesn't need warriors because it's already guarded by the other rooms we came through."

"Then maybe all the rooms inside will be safer than those others," Maria suggested hopefully.

This cheered them all. Then Penny said, "Look, there's some kind of light around the walls! It's just below the ceiling."

They looked up. A soft kind of glow extended around the top of the four walls, just under the ceiling.

"Where could that be coming from?" Penny asked curiously. "We're deep in the temple still, and I don't see how this room could have openings to the outside."

"Is that a lighter spot in the middle of the ceiling?" David asked. "Maybe a hole?"

They flashed their beams above them, and there, in the center of the ceiling, the four saw what appeared to be an opening.

"The ceiling slopes upward to meet that opening, and gets higher in the center," Penny said suddenly.

"You're right!" David said. "I think the light is coming from above, through that hole, and then it's reflecting off a row of polished stones. That's how it's getting in."

Maria noticed something else. "Look, there are doorways on both sides of this wall." She'd been flashing her light around while the others had been looking at the ceiling. Now they too looked to their left and right, and saw the openings she'd spotted.

"Which way shall we go?" Penny asked.

"We'd better make a map before we go another step," David said suddenly. "We've got to keep some record of where we've been and the turns we've taken, or we'll get lost and wander around here for a year."

"I'll make a map," Maria said. "Let me have your notebook, Penny."

Penny took off her pack, opened it, and handed Maria the notebook she used to record her photographs. "Give me some light, too," Maria asked, as she knelt on the ground, took the pen Penny gave her, and began to sketch the path they'd taken. Penny shone her flashlight on the page as Maria sketched swiftly.

"You're good at this," Penny said, as the Spanish girl sketched swiftly and accurately.

"Need any help?" Mark asked.

"No, thank you," Maria replied. "It won't take a minute."

"Then let's look around, Mark," David said, slipping off his backpack and setting it on the floor beside the girls. Mark did the same, and followed David across the room toward the door they'd seen in the far wall. The boys stopped before this door, shining their lights carefully on the stone floor.

"Looks okay," Mark said quietly.

"Sure does," David said. "Let's check the other doors."

They turned to the right and walked over to the door in that wall. Then they crossed the room and examined the other doorway.

"Nothing strange here, either," Mark said. But he noticed that David was looking along the wall to the corner of the room, where a stone statue stood guard.

"What's that?" David asked curiously, stepping quickly toward what now appeared to be a gap in the corner behind the statue. The boys came to a stop next to a narrow opening.

"I didn't see that at first," Mark said in surprise.

"Neither did I," David admitted. "But the reason we didn't is because this statue is hiding it —unless you walk around and stand here."

Carefully, they stepped closer and flashed their lights into the opening. It was perhaps seven feet high, narrow, tucked between the statue and the corner where the two walls came together.

David stuck his head inside the opening and flashed his light upward. "Here's a winding stairway going up," he said excitedly. "And there's light at the top." His voice reverberated strangely in the narrow, coffin-like compartment.

"Wonder what's up there?" Mark asked, mystified.

"We'll, we'd better check it out," David said, "'cause we've got to find ways out of here. We know we can't go back the way we came." He turned and spoke to the girls:

"Hey, we've found a small staircase going up. We'll take a look, and come right back."

"Why not wait for us?" Penny replied quickly, looking up from the page where Maria was sketching their path. "We're almost finished."

"It won't take a minute," Mark insisted. "We'll just go up to the next level and take a look."

"Okay," Penny said reluctantly. She didn't like the idea of them becoming separated. "Are you almost through?" she asked Maria.

"Almost," Maria replied. "Look at it and see what you think."

David squeezed through the opening in the wall, and began to ascend the steep narrow steps in the tube-like vertical passage. He moved slowly, carefully, flashing his light ahead and above as he climbed. He could hear Mark's footsteps behind him.

"There's a breeze coming from above," David said suddenly.

"I feel it too," Mark replied.

"I can see light," David said in another moment.

The light increased as he climbed. But it was a longer climb than he'd expected—the stairs seemed to go on and on—and he began to wonder if they shouldn't go back and wait for the girls to join them.

"How are we doing?" Mark asked from behind and below him.

"I think we're near the top, "David said, "but I wonder if we shouldn't…?"

"Great," Mark replied, not hearing David's last words as his feet scraped the stone steps. "I bet we'll find a window looking out. We can always climb down those vines on the outside if we have trouble finding a door or window."

David wondered about that. *Climb down those vines? They're probably so tangled that we'd never find a foothold. We'd be caught like flies in a spider's web.* He was about to suggest to Mark that they turn back and wait for the girls, but just then he reached the floor above. Ascending the last steps, he poked his head just above the level of the floor and flashed his light around in a quick circle.

The small room was packed with huge barrel-shaped pottery. Just ahead was a doorway. And through a matt of greenery and vines he saw daylight! "Boy," he said excitedly, "we've reached the top."

"What?" Mark replied. "The top? That's great!"

The two rushed across the room and leaned out the window; through the thick covering of vines and leaves they could see light!

Birds were chattering noisily in the thick mat of green vegetation that covered the temple.

"Listen to those birds." Mark said, "What a racket."

The birds were very noisy—so noisy, in fact, that neither Mark nor David heard Maria scream.

"WHERE'S PENNY?"

Maria stood in shock. She'd completed the quick sketch of their path into the temple. It was easy, she'd found. Then Penny had jumped up and hurried toward the corner of the room, where they'd last seen the boys.

Penny's attention had been drawn to something on the wall—the wall through which they had entered the room. "What's this?" she'd said, almost to herself, as she stepped closer to the wall and aimed her light at a spot just level with her face.

Maria had looked up just as Penny stopped, reached out, and touched the wall. Suddenly, the floor beneath Penny had swung open, and she'd tumbled with a cry out of Maria's sight.

"Penny!" Maria screamed, as she rushed to the opening through which Penny had disappeared. One panel of the flooring had swung downward as if on hinges, toward the wall. Penny had tumbled through this to the floor below.

But now, to Maria's horror, that panel in the floor began to close.

"Mark! David!" Maria screamed. "Come back!" She threw herself to the floor and pressed on the slowly rising panel as it swung back upward to close. Her flashlight was gripped in her fist with the beam pointing upward, so she could see nothing through the opening below. The stone stopped moving momentarily, then began closing again, pressing upward against her hands with irresistible force.

Sliding herself closer to the opening, praying that another stone wouldn't open beneath her, the brave girl put the weight of her body behind her arms and pressed down with all her might. "Mark! David! Hurry!" she screamed again, frantic now.

It's still open, she realized. *If only the boys will come now and help me.* She called out again and again and again. But she heard no reply. Remorselessly, the stone pressed upward, coming closer and closer to the level of the floor. Desperately, she pressed downward. But her arms began to weaken. She knew she couldn't hold the panel open much longer.

"Penny!" she cried desperately, looking into the darkness below her. There was no answer.

"Penny! Answer me!" Maria cried again.

Silence. Though the panel was still half a foot from being closed, there was no sound from below.

On the level above, Mark and David had peered through gaps in the matted vines and leaves and seen the brightness of the clear day.

"We can cut a hole through that stuff if we have to," Mark said optimistically, "and climb down the outside of the temple. That is, if we can't find another door out of here."

"Well, there have *got* to be other doors out of here!" David said. "We'd have a tough time climbing down that slanting web of vines to the ground, Mark. So would the girls."

"You're right," Mark agreed. "But I was just thinking that this is always an option. Maybe I should cut a hole in this now." He drew his long knife from its sheath, reached through the window in the stone wall, grabbed a vine, and sliced it through. In a few moments he'd made a sizeable hole.

"Watch for snakes. And spiders," David cautioned.

"Easier said than done," Mark replied. He continued to cut the vines, making the hole wider. "Hey! I've scared the birds. They're quiet now."

"That's big enough," David said. "Let me go through."

"Nothing doing," Mark retorted, slipping his knife back into the sheath. "I cut it, I'll go through it. Give me a boost."

David cupped his hands, Mark put his foot in the ready-made stirrup, grabbed a handful of vines, and pulled himself through. Working himself into a sitting position, he turned, his upper body completely outside the carpet-like covering of tangled vines, and looked around.

"Wow," he said, squinting into the sudden bright sunlight. "What a view!"

"What do you see?" David asked eagerly.

"A world with sunlight," Mark said instantly. "That's the best thing. Man, am I tired of groping around in the dark."

"Then move over and I'll…" David never finished. With the birds suddenly silent, he had just heard Maria's desperate scream.

"Hey, Maria's yelling! We've got to get back!" David said as he whirled and ran to the narrow stairway in the corner of the room.

"What?" Mark said, whipping his body around in the thick vines and leaves. "I'm coming…"

Mark didn't complete his sentence either. As he twisted himself around, a section of vines tore away under the weight of his body. Suddenly, he tumbled downward, falling backwards into a mass of dead leaves that covered a ledge some feet underneath the matted vine blanket that covered the temple.

David was already into the coffin-like spiral passage, moving downward as rapidly as he dared. He never heard Mark's fall, nor did he hear Mark call out. *Careful!* David reminded himself, as he squeezed through the narrow passage, trying to see what the beam of his light was showing, but finding this difficult because of the steep angle.

I don't need to break an ankle here, he thought. He slowed down.

"I'm coming, Maria," he called.

But it was with agonizing slowness that he worked his way down, shoulders brushing the stone walls, feet groping carefully for a foothold on the incredibly narrow steep steps. Suddenly his foot missed a step and his body flew forward. Throwing out his hands, he caught himself on the wall so close to his face. Bracing himself there for a moment, he felt around for the step with his foot. He found this finally, and, a bit shaken, resumed his descent. He gripped the light in his right hand, and held his left in front of his face, ready to brace against the wall again if he missed another step.

"Maria," he called, "I'm coming!"

"Hurry!" she yelled back. "I can't hold this open any more!"

Hold what open? David wondered desperately.

Finally he reached the floor, rushed from the narrow vertical tunnel, and spotted her just a few feet away. And then he understood: Maria was lying face down on the floor, pressing with all her might against a stone panel that was pushing slowly upward against her hands!

David dashed to her side, threw himself to the floor, and shoved downward with all his might.

"Oh, thank the Lord you came in time," she gasped. "Penny fell through the floor, and the stone was closing back. I called and called but she doesn't answer!"

"Penny," David called sharply, then again, "Penny!"

"A stone in the floor gave way, that's why she fell through," Maria said, her dark eyes showing the agony of her soul. "Then that stone started moving back upward. It must be on a hinge, with weights making it close. I called you and Mark, but you didn't answer either."

"We couldn't hear you until those birds stopped chattering," David replied. Then he called for Penny again.

The stone panel now moved slowly down under the relentless pressure of David's arms. Soon it was hanging vertically on its hinges. Then David felt the pressure stop.

"I think it'll stay," he said gratefully. "It must have counterweights to make it close like that." He remembered reading about the clever traps by which ancient peoples guarded their temples and tombs, traps that still worked centuries after they were made. Now he wondered how they'd ever get out of such a place.

But the immediate problem was the plight of Penny. Quickly he thrust his head and arms through the opening, and swept his flashlight in a quick search of the floor below.

"There she is!" he said. Then his body stiffened in shock. "But she's not moving."

"What?" Maria cried. "Oh, David, what's the matter?"

"I don't know," David replied, "but I'm going down. Go get Mark's pack and bring me the rope. Hurry, I'll make sure this panel doesn't close."

FLIGHT FROM THE TEMPLE

Maria rose and rushed to the pack Mark had dropped to the floor. Opening this frantically, she pulled out the large coil of rope, and dashed back to David.

"Where's Mark," she asked as she handed him the rope.

"He should be right behind me," David said, quickly unwinding the cord that held the coiled rope together. "Watch that panel while I unwind this. Tell me if it starts to close again."

Swiftly he undid the coil, grabbed one end, and ran over to the statue that hid the stairway. Throwing the rope around the base of the stone figure, he quickly tied a strong knot. Then he rushed back to join Maria. He tossed the remainder of the coil down into the darkness, then began to fashion the rope in ways too quick for Maria to follow.

David leaned into the opening again and flashed the light on Penny. She lay on her side, not moving. He swept the beam around the floor below for a final check and saw that the room was covered by a thick carpet of tangled vines. Along two walls were rows of what appeared to be stone or clay jars, some of them three or four feet tall. Penny was lying by one of these walls.

Suddenly, something moved at the edge of David's vision. Startled, he swept the light back again toward the far wall to his left, and his face froze in horror.

The six-foot long thick-bodied green snake was slithering slowly toward the unconscious girl.

A green mamba!

THE GREEN MAMBA

Outside the temple, under the blanket-like carpet of matted vegetation, Mark struggled to climb back to the window from which he'd fallen. He was almost suffocated by the tangled leaves and branches as he clambered slowly up. Gradually he worked his way up toward the window.

When he grabbed the edge of the opening through which he'd tumbled, however, the vines tore away again, causing him to fall back halfway to the ledge on which he'd first struck. Desperately he began again the agonizing struggle back, hampered by the incredibly twisted mass of vines and leaves. Finally, he reached the enlarged opening.

With great care he reached out and seized the strongest vines he could find. Then, very slowly, he lifted himself through the opening, bracing his feet in the matted vines as he reached for another grip. Pulling himself slowly upward, he finally reached the window.

"David," Mark yelled. "Give me a hand!"

There was no answer.

Mark gripped the stone ledge and pulled himself slowly up to the window. Then he climbed through, and stepped into the room. He reached for his flashlight—it was gone, fallen from his pocket as he'd tumbled through the vines. His knife also was gone.

"David," he yelled again, moving swiftly toward the coffin-like tunnel through which he and his friend had climbed from the level below. The light from the window was bright enough to enable him to find the stairway. Reaching this, he looked below into darkness.

"Oh, Lord," he prayed fervently, "please help me get down."

Slowly he began the descent, groping with hands and feet, moving with infinite care, wondering all the while where David had gone. *This place is like a tomb,* he thought, fighting off feelings of suffocating in the constricted vertical tunnel.

It was cool in the passageway, but Mark was sweating as he made his way down, step by careful step. He could see nothing now, not even the glow from the light that had filtered into the room above him. Through utter darkness he moved cautiously downward, feeling with his feet, holding the walls with his hands, bracing himself against a sudden miss-step.

His foot slipped on the slick stone step and he fell.

In the room below, David thrust the flashlight into his pocket, and grabbed Maria's hand in which she held her light. Aiming this at the huge mamba, he said, "Keep the light on that snake."

She cried out in horror at the sight of the long thick reptile that was moving toward the still form of Penny.

Then David gripped the rope with both hands and went head first through the opening, turning over as he descended rapidly hand over hand. He dropped the last few feet, hitting the floor beside the fallen girl.

The snake had halted momentarily as Maria's light illumined its face. Then the animal's thick head snapped back toward David as it heard the boy land beside Penny.

For a moment David and the snake stared at each other, neither moving. Then David stepped quickly toward the row of thick jars against the wall, lifted one with both hands, stepped back past Penny, and tossed it at the approaching mamba. While the jar was still in the air, he whirled around and grabbed another, brought this forward, and threw it after the first.

The first big jar fell just in front of the snake, shattering, causing the reptile to halt as it was struck by shards of broken pottery. The second jar struck the wall beside and above the mamba and crashed in thick pieces on its head. The animal darted forward.

Twice more David grabbed and threw the jars, as fast as he could reach for them. Then one of them appeared to do some damage. It struck the animal's head as it slithered along the floor, and seemed to stun the creature.

But David knew that it would take a lot more than a few blows to injure a snake that size. Their bodies were incredibly tough, and a reptile this big would not be stopped long.

Maria, shuddering with fear for David and Penny, kept her grip on the flashlight, and kept its beam centered on the animal's now motionless head.

Emboldened, David reached for another row of jars. These were smaller, and as he picked the first one from the ground he realized that this was made of stone, not clay. He lifted the heavy vessel above his head, moved forward toward the seemingly stunned animal, and threw it down in an arc toward the deadly creature.

"David, you're too close!" Maria called suddenly.

David knew he was. But he had to hit that snake. The heavy stone vessel caught the snake's head flat on the floor, and this seemed to do damage. The animal's tail whipped around suddenly - then its body was still.

Swiftly, David stepped back to Penny. Kneeling beside her, he lifted her head. Maria switched the beam back for a moment, and in its light David was able to see Penny's eyes flutter open.

"What happened?" Penny asked feebly.

"The floor gave way, and you fell through," David said, his heart leaping with joy that she had come awake.

"Can you get up?" he asked. *I've got to get her out of here before that snake revives,* he thought.

"I'll try," she said. Shakily she sat up; then she let him help her stand. She swayed, leaning against him, and he held her with his arms around her.

"David," Mark's strong voice boomed in the stone chamber. "What can I do?"

Mark had caught himself against the wall of the passageway as he fell, stumbled a few steps, and then had fallen out into the room. Seeing Maria's crouched form faintly outlined against the light of her flashlight, he'd limped over to her and thrown himself flat. Quickly, Maria told him what was had happened.

"Mark, Penny fell through the floor. There's a horrible huge snake there. David stunned it, I think—but we've got to get her out of there!"

David glanced directly up to see the faces of his two friends in the reflected light.

"Penny's still groggy," David called back. "We've got to lift her out of here! I'll make a loop in this rope for her to sit in. Then I'll climb back and we'll bring her up!"

Swiftly, David reached for the line and knotted a loop for Penny. Helping her into this, he glanced back at the snake, which was still illumined in the beam of Maria's light. The animal was not moving.

"Hold on, Penny," he said. "I'm going up; then Mark and I will pull you up. Just hold tight to the line and don't let go."

"Okay," she said feebly.

For good measure, David coiled the rope around her waist as well. Then he tied a swift knot to keep this in place. "I'm coming up," David called. He grabbed the rope above his head and went up hand over hand, faster than he'd ever climbed in his life. Crawling through the opening, he reached down and swiftly gathered in the loose coil of rope until it went taut. *The pressure of her weight on the rope will keep that panel from moving back,* he thought.

"Ready, Penny?" he called.

"Yes," she said in a faint voice.

"Just hold tight. Don't let go for any reason! We've got to get you out of that room."

"All right," she said.

"Mark," David said, "wrap this around your waist, then walk away. I'll pull too."

Mark jumped up, wrapped the rope around his waist, gripped it in his strong hands, leaned against the weight of Penny's body at the end of the rope, and began to walk backwards into the dark. David gripped the rope behind Mark and pulled with him.

Penny began to rise from the floor. Then she was off the ground, moving slowly upward.

"The snake's coming!" Maria cried suddenly.

STRANGE LIGHT

"Keep moving!" David said, leaving Mark and rushing back to the hole in the floor.

Throwing himself down, he peered below. Penny, sitting in the loop of the rope, was several feet above the ground, but still too close to the floor, and almost within reach of the approaching green mamba.

"Back, Mark!" David yelled, as he jumped up, gripped the rope and added his strength to Mark's.

Slowly Penny was lifted up, closer and closer to David. Then David reached down and grabbed her right wrist. She gripped her hand around his wrist, groped with her other hand for the edge of the trap door, and was pulled into the room. Then she collapsed on the floor.

David threw himself flat and reached through the opening for the edge of the stone panel. Grabbing this, he gave it a pull; the counterweights went into action, and slowly the panel began to close.

David's last sight of the huge snake gave him a shock—the deadly animal was right below the opening, head lifted high, looking up at him! *We got Penny out just in time,* he thought. Then the panel closed and David saw the snake no more. He shuddered at her narrow escape.

Mark unwound the rope from his waist, rushed to Penny, and helped her to sit up. Then he sat beside her and held her in his arms. David and Maria clustered around in the small area of light illumined by Maria's flashlight.

"Any hurts?" Mark asked.

"I think I've got a bump on my head," Penny said slowly, "but I don't think anything else is wrong. So there was a snake down there too?"

"There was," Maria replied. "David went down the rope and threw jars at it and made it stop."

Penny tried to comprehend what had happened as David got out his light and shined it on her head. He felt her hair and found a swelling on the left side of her head.

"Well, you've got a little bump, but if that's all then we can thank the Lord for His protection! You fell all the way to the floor."

"What's on that floor she fell on?" Maria asked.

"It felt like dead vines and leaves," David said. "That's what kept her from getting hurt. Boy, that was close."

"How about a lunch break?" Mark inquired. He knew that Penny could use something to drink, and he thought they'd all be cheered by food.

"Can we get out of this room first?" Maria asked. Suddenly she felt cold; she shivered.

"Sure," Mark said. "You ready, Penny?"

"Yes," she replied. "I feel okay now. Thanks everyone." She looked at David then, but didn't know what to say.

"Anyone got an extra light?" Mark asked.

"I do," David replied. He took a flashlight out of his pack and handed it over.

"Let's keep going, then," Mark agreed. The four headed for the door opposite the one through which they'd come. Mark led this time, the girls followed, and David came last.

"Watch out at the entrance," Maria warned. "We don't want to step on another trap."

"That's the truth." Mark agreed. He stopped before the door and they all studied the floor in the light of his and Maria's lights.

"Looks okay to me," David said.

"Me too," Mark agreed. "I'll go through first. You three stay here." He stepped quickly through the door and passed into the next room. "Hey, this is neat," he said. "Come on in."

The girls went swiftly through the door and David followed them. Now they found themselves standing in a circular room. A series of stone benches was arranged in semi-circles, facing a low table at the far end of the room. High on the round wall above them was a row of polished panels, bright as glass, and from these came a diffuse golden light. A bright yellow glow enfolded the table around which the benches were curved.

"Wow," Penny said. "Look at the lighting in *this* room."

"It's got to be coming from the outside, above that row of polished stones," Mark observed. "There must be an opening to the sky above them."

"But I wonder how many times the light is bent and reflected before it reaches those panels?" Penny asked, fascinated. Her strength was returning now, and her curiosity was aroused. The others were thrilled to see that she was bouncing back.

"I don't know, but I bet we can figure it out while we sit on those benches and eat," Mark suggested.

They laughed at this and it seemed to relieve the tension they'd all felt. They parked themselves on two of the benches near the table, and opened their packs. Mark and David then told the girls what they'd found at the top of the winding staircase. Then Mark told how he'd fallen through the matted vegetation after David had rushed back to join the girls.

"I couldn't understand why you boys didn't answer when I called," Maria said, "and now I know. Those birds made too much noise—until they heard Mark cut the vines."

Mark had another thought. "Penny, what kind of a stone was that you stepped on, when the floor opened? We were in such a hurry to get out of that room that we didn't look at it."

"It was just like all the others on the floor," she replied. "I didn't see anything suspicious at all. I didn't want you boys to get too far away from Maria and me, so I hurried to the place where I'd last seen you. But I think I got closer to that wall than you did, then all I remember was falling." She felt the bump on her head. "Guess I hit my head on the wall when I fell through."

"Maybe that was a good thing," Mark suggested, "'cause you were so relaxed when you hit the bottom that you didn't break anything."

"There's more than one kind of trap in this place," David said soberly.

The others looked at him, not knowing what to say.

"How can we spot them in time?" Maria asked, breaking the silence finally.

After a moment, David said carefully, "Well, the first trap we found had a different type of stone in front of the door."

"But I noticed that other doors had that same color stone in front of them, David," Penny said quickly. "Not the next ones we went through, but the doors on the side of the room. And we don't know if they were traps or not. If not, that may just be an artistic touch by the builders. I don't think the color will always tell us."

Mark agreed. "Well, that trap was next to the wall, Penny said. So maybe we've just got to stay away from the walls."

They fell silent then, eating their sandwiches and drinking the water they'd brought in their daypacks. Suddenly Penny sat up straight and looked around.

"Look, the light's changed. It's lighter now."

The others glanced around in surprise. "Penny's right," Maria said. "But how could that be?"

"I bet our eyes have just gotten used to the light," Mark observed. "We're not using our flashlights, and we're just accustomed to the light that's coming from those places in the ceiling and striking those polished stones."

"Maybe," Penny said in a puzzled tone. But she wasn't convinced. *I think there is more light here,* she thought. *But I can't imagine how that could happen. Surely there's no one here but us, and we're not near the source of the light.*

Had she heard voices from the opening in the ceiling? She rose and walked closer to the stone table. *Are those men's voices above me?*

"Did any of you hear people talking?" she asked suddenly.

Mark, Maria, and David looked at her in surprise. Then they looked at each other.

"Do you think you hit your head harder than we thought?" Mark asked with a smile.

"No I don't!" Penny said emphatically. "Do you think there could be anyone above us in the temple? Maybe they made the light change somehow."

"Well, who could be here?" Mark answered. "Except for Colonel Lamumba, his men, and Dad's men, we're probably the only people in the world who know that this temple exists."

Penny looked over at Maria. The Spanish girl could see the worry in her friend's eyes. *Penny's a photographer,* Maria reminded herself. *She really notices things better than we do. But what does it mean? I thought I heard something too, but I'm not sure.* She shrugged her shoulders and moved back to join the others.

Three levels above the four teens, Hoffmann and his men gazed in wonder at the amazing arrangement of angled polished stone mirrors in the room. The mirrors, set upright at angles on flat stones, were arranged in a large circle around a wide, round hole, cut in the floor. They were angled so as to catch the light that came from several openings in the ceiling, and reflect this to the polished stones in the sides of the hole that led to the level below. In spite of the vegetation that covered the temple, gaps in the leaves and vines allowed light to enter several of the side-openings in small structures atop the building, and this light was passed down to rooms below by the clever system devised by the mysterious ancient builders.

Walther began experimenting with the angle of the polished mirrors, shoving a couple of the mirrors into different positions in their circular stone track. The room had an eerie feeling to it, and for some reason all of the men had begun to lower their voices when they'd entered.

"So that's how they got light into these lower rooms!" Hoffmann said. "Those people were pretty smart!"

"Whoever *they* were," Stefan replied. He was getting claustrophobic now, and longed to finish this inside work and get back to the open sky.

"Well, *whoever* they were, they sure knew a lot about building and lighting," Hoffmann commented. "But we're interested in their treasure, not their lighting. And this isn't their treasure room. We've come too high up, I think. Let's go to a lower level. We'll keep searching each level until we find the gold and jewels."

The four men picked up their bags of equipment and made their way to the narrow stairway, which had led them up to this room.

THE CHARIOT OF
THE PHARAOH

"Well, that makes me feel like a new man," Mark exclaimed, as he finished his sandwich and his share of the brownies Penny had made for their lunch. "Those were great, Penny! How do you feel?"

"Fine," she replied brightly, smiling up at him. "Honest, everybody, I'm okay now. I was stunned for a while, but now I'm ready to go." *Maybe I didn't hear people talking after all,* she thought. *Maybe my head was still ringing.* She decided to forget the voices she thought she'd heard.

"Well, I'll mark this room on my map," Maria said, "then we'll know where we've been at least, even if we don't know where we're going!" She laughed, and they laughed with her. The meal had made them all feel better.

"Let's make a ninety degree turn and head deeper into the temple," David suggested.

"Why ninety degrees?" Mark asked innocently. "Why not forty-five?"

"I figured you'd remember a right angle turn easier, that's why," David said. "Besides, it'll look neater on Maria's map. And it'll also bring us closer to the other side of the temple. We can't go back the way we came in, remember, so we've got to get out the other side."

"Well, there's only three doors in this room," Maria observed. "But the one to our left leads to the other side of the temple."

"Let's go," David said. "But let me scout that door before we go through it."

"We'd better start conserving out batteries," Mark said. "We don't know how long it'll take us to get out of here."

"Good idea," David said. "I'll use mine right now, and you use yours, Maria. Penny, you and Mark keep yours in reserve."

"You brought along some of those light sticks, didn't you?" Penny asked.

"We did," David replied. "I think we're in good shape, but Mark's right. We want to keep a reserve."

The four shouldered their daypacks and followed David to the door Maria had pointed out.

"See anything that looks different, Penny?" David asked, as they approached the door.

"No."

"What about the walls, and over the door?" Mark said. David and Maria flashed their beams up the walls, searching carefully, and then aimed them over the door.

"No big round stone wheels over this door," Penny said.

"It looks okay," David concluded. "Wait here and I'll go in."

He stepped into the room while they waited. "Wow!" he exclaimed. "Come on in and look at these hieroglyphics!"

As the others entered, David walked farther into the room and stopped before a freestanding wall that blocked his path. About twenty-five feet wide, it stretched all the way to the ceiling, and was covered with brightly colored paintings. To go further into the room, he would have to go around to the left or right of this wall.

This is curious, he thought.

David flashed his beam to the left. All he could see of that wall, too, was covered with the same brightly painted hieroglyphics. Looking to his right, he saw that it too was covered with identical decorations. He turned to his left and came to the edge of the wall. Stepping around this, he saw behind the wall a monstrous seated figure - a man's body, with a crocodile's head. The figure appeared to be covered with gold leaf.

"Come see this," he called.

Quickly the others came into the room around the wall with its strange hieroglyphics, and joined him.

"'Wow' is right!" Mark exclaimed, as he came to a halt beside David.

"But this is just like the temple we saw in Egypt," Penny exclaimed, eyes wide with surprise and puzzlement.

"How could that kind of art be here in East Africa?" Maria asked.

"There was a lot of trade between Egypt and East Africa in ancient times," David answered. "And this sure looks like the stuff we saw in Pharaoh's tomb - especially this crocodile-headed man. Remember, Penny, that ugly idol in the treasure room?"

"I sure do," she said, "and it gave me the creeps. And it does now. It looks—no it *feels* evil. And that's what Colonel Lamumba told Daddy, that we'd maybe see some Egyptian-type art in this temple."

"It does look hateful," Maria said, shuddering, as she moved closer to Penny and stared at the frightful statue.

"Its eyes seem to be looking straight at you, no matter where you stand," Mark observed quietly. He'd stepped away from David several feet and it still seemed as if the crocodile's eye was following him.

"But look at these other images," Maria said, awed at another sight beyond the ugly threatening statue. She flashed her light past the crocodile. And there, before the stunned eyes of the teens, was a row of smaller images, each with crocodile heads and fabulous, gold-painted bodies. Jewels were set in the gold, and these sparkled brilliantly in the beam from Maria's light. The darkness hovered all around them, and the light flashing from the jewels and gold leaped out at them like flames.

"Wow," Penny said, as she and Maria walked over to the nearest gold-covered figure. "Look at these!"

The beams from their flashlights made weird shadows appear and disappear behind the statues. Mark and David walked with the girls to study the smaller gold-covered figures. And then, the four teens seemed to forget all about time. They wandered past statue after statue, each covered with gold, each studded with precious gems. Behind these was a second standing wall near the back of the room, one identical to the one they'd just come around. On this wall they found more of the mysterious hieroglyphics rising from the floor and reaching to the ceiling.

"What can all these symbols mean?" Mark asked no one in particular, as he studied the strange designs.

"Keno would know!" Penny answered. "Remember, he could sight-read the hieroglyphics in Pharaoh's tomb, and these look just the same." She quickly told Maria of their Egyptian friend, the translator with whom they'd worked as they had explored Pharaoh's tomb in Egypt so many weeks before.

"I wish Keno were here now," David said. He had wandered past the statues, stepped around the second standing wall, and disappeared from sight. But they could hear him clearly in the stone chamber. "What a story these walls would tell us!" he said, as he walked to the far wall of the room. Then he whistled in amazement. "Hey, come look at this - a chariot!"

The three rushed around the standing wall and joined him.

"I can't believe it!" Penny said, in awe of what she saw. Along the back wall of the room was a long mural; on this, brightly painted marching men advanced to battle. In their midst was a chariot with two regal figures standing, one holding the horse's reins, the other a spear.

"Look at that," David said in a hushed tone. "Just like the one in Pharaoh's tomb!"

"You mean you've seen this before?" Maria asked incredulously.

"Well," Penny replied, her eyes wide with amazement, "this is the same picture we saw in that underground tomb in Egypt."

Penny and David and Mark were thunderstruck at seeing a scene so familiar to them, a scene that brought back sinister memories of the time when they'd been trapped underground in an ancient Egyptian tomb.

"That's the chariot of the Pharaoh, all right," David said emphatically.

The four teenagers stood in silence for a moment, studying this strange encounter with the familiar picture. Surrounded by the heavy darkness, barely visible to each other in the limited light from the flashlights in David's and Maria's hands, they pondered the sinister scene.

Suddenly they were stunned by the gruff sound of men's voices. They stiffened in horror.

"Who could that be?" Penny whispered, shocked.

"Douse the light, Maria," David said at once, as he switched off his own. The four teens huddled together in absolute blackness against the wall, as the sounds of voices drew closer.

"They're coming this way," Mark whispered.

Now the four could see light seeping around both sides of the wall behind which they stood. Loud voices rang through the stone chamber.

"They're speaking German!" David whispered.

"IS THERE NO WAY OUT?"

The four clustered close against the wall, hardly daring to breathe. The sound of the footsteps and voices grew louder. Then they heard the men exclaim in astonishment as they turned their flashlights on the first wall and saw its hieroglyphics.

"Look at that!" a voice said in astonishment.

"That's Hoffmann!" Penny whispered in her brother's ear. She was horrified.

"Impossible," Mark whispered back. "How could Hoffmann be here?"

The men were speaking loudly on the other side of the two walls that separated them, and thus could not hear the quiet whispers of the teens.

"I know that voice," Penny whispered again. "I'll always know his voice! Oh, how can we get away from him?" She turned to David, leaned her face close to his, and whispered, "What are they saying?"

"They're just marveling at those weird pictures," David whispered back, trying to keep his voice steady.

We're trapped! he thought to himself.

The men on the other side of the wall were speaking more loudly now, astonished at the strange sights that were revealed in the beams of their lights. Then the teens heard an African voice, asking his comrades to speak in English. The Germans complied, and soon the men were in loud and animated conversation, drowning out any possibility of their hearing the muted whispering of the teens behind the wall.

"Is there a door on this side of the room?" Mark whispered, leaning close to David.

"I didn't see one," David replied. "Not on this wall. Just the mural."

"I didn't see any door to our left," Maria added despondently.

"There was one on the right," Penny said.

"But we can't go that way now!" Mark whispered. "If they come around that standing wall they'll see us at once!"

"Is there no way out?" Maria asked frantically.

"Crowd around me and give me cover," David whispered suddenly. "I'm going to use my light and study this mural again - I saw something."

"But those men will see the light," Penny whispered.

"I'll hold my hand over the glass," David replied, "and just let a sliver of light through. Hurry! Get on both sides of me while I turn it on, so no light can escape behind us!"

The men's voices sounded suddenly closer.

FLIGHT FROM THE TEMPLE

"They've come around that first wall," Maria whispered. "I think they're standing in front of that statue, just like we did!"

Their hearts sank. Now, only the free standing wall on this side of the room kept them from being discovered. Now the men were marveling at the treasure they saw; the statues with inlaid gems!

"Quick," Mark whispered. "Get close and cover David."

Mark and Penny pressed close to David's right; Maria did the same on his left. David covered the lens of his flashlight with his hand and switched it on, letting only a tiny sliver of light escape between his fingers.

"What are you looking for?" Maria asked.

"I think I know!" Penny said suddenly. "The hub of the chariot's wheel!"

"That's right," David whispered back. "But I can't find it!"

"Down a little," Mark said. "You're too high."

The tiny beam escaping between David's fingers was so small he could barely make out the features of the mural as he searched frantically for the wheel. At Mark's suggestion, however, he moved the light down and found a spoke. Quickly he moved the narrow beam of light down the spoke until he came to the hub.

"That's it," Penny said. "That's it, David! Oh, do you think it'll work?"

Utterly mystified by this talk about the chariot and its wheel, Maria kept silent. She knew that her three friends had experienced things that summer that taught them many lessons, some of which they'd already shared with her. She also knew that they talked over these experiences, studied them, in fact, considering how they might have acted more alertly and more quickly to escape the dangerous situations they'd encountered. Now she remained silent while the three made their plans.

David placed his left hand against the hub of the chariot wheel. "I'm going to switch off this light and hand it to you, Penny," he whispered, as quietly as he could. "Here, take it while you can see."

Penny reached for his hand. David switched off the light, and she took the flashlight from him. Then David placed both hands against the hub of the chariot's wheel, and began to push.

"Move back a bit," he whispered suddenly, "we don't know which way this wall might move. But don't make a sound."

The men's voices were loud now, frighteningly so, as they discussed the surprising statue that had astonished the teenagers just a short while before. Then the sound of their steps and voices became even louder as they walked farther into the room, whistling in amazement at the gold-covered statues that now leaped before them in the powerful beams of their lights. And this light flashed around both sides of the wall behind which the teens were hiding.

Soon they would be discovered!

David pushed harder against the panel of stone. It didn't budge.

"Is it moving?" Mark whispered anxiously.

"Not yet," David said. "Pray, all of you."

Suddenly David felt the wall move in so quickly that he almost fell. Recovering rapidly, he asked Penny for the light. She reached for his shoulder, and then found his outstretched hand.

Instantly he covered the glass with his hand, flipped the switch, and opened a narrow slit between his fingers.

The panel had moved back, and revealed an opening in the wall, just like the openings in Pharaoh's tomb!

"It's open," Penny whispered. "Oh, David, you found it!"

"Go in, David," Mark whispered at once. "You girls follow him. I'll be right behind."

David crawled swiftly into the opening, followed by Maria and Penny. Mark came last. David had stayed close to the opening, and when Mark came through, he let him pass. Then David put his hands on the edge of the panel that had swung open into the room, and began to push it back. To his relief, it moved smoothly, easily. When he felt it close, he ran his fingers along the wall to make sure it was flush. Then he turned, switched on the light, and moved past the girls and Mark. He flashed the light ahead and stood up.

The tunnel was narrow, no more than five feet wide. And it was not tall. David's head almost touched the ceiling.

"At least we're safe here," Maria whispered gratefully, as she rose to her feet with Mark and Penny.

"Not yet, we're not," David said at once. "We've got to get away from that wall. Hoffmann will remember where to push to open the panel. That's how he and his men chased us in Pharaoh's tomb."

This shocked Maria, but Mark and Penny were already aware of their danger. They too were ready to move.

"Lead off, David," Mark whispered urgently. "You girls follow him."

Quickly, David started down the narrow tunnel. Penny was next, Maria came after her, and Mark came last. David was careful to flash the light upwards every few feet. He didn't want to smash his face against any stone projecting down from the low ceiling.

Maria had turned her light on also, and aimed this at her feet as they walked, to help Mark as he brought up the rear of the solemn procession. They didn't speak as they walked quickly through the blackness. No one said what they all feared—that at any moment they might hear those men open the panel in the wall and come after them.

They walked for maybe sixty feet, when suddenly David stopped, causing Penny to bump into him. "What's the matter?" she whispered anxiously.

"There are passages on each side of the tunnel," he said. "I don't know which way to go."

"Does it still go straight ahead?" Mark asked. Standing behind the two girls, he couldn't see past David.

"Yeah," David said. "It goes straight ahead, and it goes to both sides."

"Well," Mark suggested, "maybe— "

But David interrupted him. "Wait! In a few feet, the path on the left starts to go down."

"What about the others?" Penny asked.

David flashed his light to his right. Maria did also, and she was the first to see the steps there.

"This one goes up. I see steps," she said.

David moved a couple of feet forward so that the others could stand with him in the narrow crossway.

Then Penny said thoughtfully: "Well, we've come up a couple of levels already, haven't we? I mean, we were above the ground when we climbed up those vines to get into the temple, and we came up some stairs a few rooms back."

"That's right," David said. "So you think that if we go left, down those steps, we might get back to the ground level?"

"I think so," she said.

"That's a good idea," Mark said.

"I think she's right!" David answered. "Let's go left."

"Whatever we do, we've got to stay together!" Maria insisted. "We just can't let ourselves get separated."

"You're right," Mark replied, giving her a reassuring hug around the shoulders. "Don't worry, we won't leave you girls again!"

"Let's go," David said, "Use your lights going down these steps."

They all turned on their lights and followed David.

"They're pretty steep," he said. "Be careful." Slowly he led them down the sharp descent.

"It's colder here," Penny said suddenly.

They all felt the cold breeze rising from the stairwell below.

"Boy, I bet we're heading for an opening," Mark whispered.

"But don't forget, we're still probably near the middle of the temple," David reminded him. "Maria's map showed the way we'd come, and it was pretty much straight ahead after we'd made that first right angle turn."

"Yeah, but a cool breeze means air's moving, and that's got to be coming from the outside," Mark said encouragingly.

"Maybe those men won't see the wheel," Penny said hopefully.

They were all speaking in very low voices.

"Maybe they won't," David replied hesitantly. But he was afraid that Hoffmann would recognize that mural as being similar to the wall drawings in Pharaoh's tomb. And if he once saw that chariot, he'd remember the way to open the panel.

David didn't mention what was in fact in all of their minds: *Had Hoffmann and his men heard them crawl through the opening in the wall, and close it behind them?*

We've got to move fast, he knew.

"Watch it!" David said suddenly, coming to a halt. "Wow, I almost smashed my head on that rock." He flashed the beam of his light upward, and the others saw the sudden drop in the ceiling.

"Want to change places?" Mark asked quickly. "I'm not as tall as you."

"I'm okay," David replied. "I'll just be careful. Thanks."

Suddenly he had a terrible thought: *What if we reach the end of this passage, and find a door we can't open?*

"THERE'S SOMEONE IN THIS ROOM!"

"I tell you I heard voices," Stefan insisted angrily. "I thought I heard them when we first got in the room, but I wasn't sure. Then I heard them when you two were talking about these pictures. Someone was whispering—two people, in fact. There's someone in this room."

"Let's check," Hoffmann snapped tersely. "Walther, you and Kala go to the right. Stefan, you come with me." The four men moved swiftly behind the powerful beams of their lights toward the wall ahead. They swept past the wall, ready to fight—but all they saw were the idols and the next standing wall. Now they were blinding each other with their lights.

"Put that light down," Hoffmann said angrily, "You're wrecking my vision!"

"There's no one here anyway," Walther said, lowering his light, looking scornfully at Stefan.

"I tell you, I *heard* people whispering," Stefan insisted.

"Well, where are they then?" Walther asked, sneering.

"I don't know where they are, but I know I heard them." Stefan was utterly baffled, and angered that the other thought he was a fool. *I know I heard people whispering,* he said to himself. *Where could they have gone?*

Walther cursed, turned, and walked back into the room to look at the huge statue of the gold-covered crocodile-headed idol. Kala hesitated a moment, then followed him. Hoffmann turned and looked at Stefan.

"You're sure?" Hoffmann asked quietly.

"I'm sure," Stefan answered firmly.

"Let's look for a door, then," Hoffmann said, turning his light on the wall, and moving the beam systematically left and right. Stefan did the same, but there was no sign of a door.

Suddenly Hoffmann gasped. His beam had fallen on the chariot.

"I can't believe this," he said, moving closer. He pored over the details of the chariot, moved the light downward to the wheel, and gasped again. "You may have been right, Stefan." He said, centering his light on the hub of the wheel. "Walther, Kala!"

At once Walther and Kala left the crocodile-headed idol, came around the standing wall, and stood beside Hoffmann and Stefan.

"Look at that," Hoffmann said tensely.

"It's a chariot," Walther said, unimpressed. Kala said nothing.

"Don't you remember what I told you about that temple in Egypt?" Hoffmann asked.

"When you were in Egypt, I was in jail," Walther reminded him.

Hoffmann ignored the bitterness in Walther's tone. "But I told you how Daring's kids got away from us in that Egyptian tomb. And a chariot was the key. There was a chariot like this in that tomb, and it covered a secret panel that opened into another room. If Stefan heard people whispering behind this wall, and they're not here now, then this is how they got away."

All of Hoffmann's anger against those American teenagers who'd ruined his plans that entire summer boiled up in his mind now.

"Move back," he commanded. "Aim your light at that wheel—at the hub. And watch."

Kneeling on the floor before the wheel, which was now illumined by the beams of the flashlights, he placed his hands on the hub of the chariot's wheel, and began to push.

Nothing happened.

Walther sneered. Hoffmann redoubled his efforts, and to the astonishment of his comrades, a panel in the wall swung open.

"You were right, Stefan," Hoffmann said, lowering his voice now. "There *were* people in this room. And this is how they got away." He flashed his light into the tunnel. "I don't see anyone now. That tunnel seems to go a long way. Maybe it's got turns and they took one of those."

"What will we do now, Hoffmann?" Kala asked quietly. "We've found the treasure. Will we leave it to go chase someone we haven't even seen? We came for the treasure and we found it."

"Would you want to let these people get away, and maybe jump us when we're not expecting them?" Hoffmann replied.

"But we don't know who they are or if they were really there," Kala said quietly.

Walther entered the discussion. "It's going to take us a lot of trips to bring out this treasure. If there's anyone else around, we can't leave them free to ambush us while we're carrying the treasure to the plane. We should go after them now, Hoffmann, and put them out of our way."

"But we have no idea where this tunnel leads," Kala said with quiet intensity. "Nor what we will find if we follow it, Walther. This temple is huge—we could wander around all day and not encounter those people—if they are really there. I say we should get to work, stick together, bring out these jewels and gold, and load them in the plane as fast as we can. We can leave one man to guard the plane while the others come back for more."

"It's bad tactics to leave an unknown enemy around," Hoffmann said decisively. "We'll go after them, chase them down, put them out of the way, and *then* come back for the loot. That way, we won't leave any witnesses."

Kala sighed, but spoke no more.

"Let's go," Hoffmann said. "But don't make any noise."

Flashlight in hand, Hoffmann crawled through the opening. Walther came next, then Stefan. They too held lights. Kala was last, a light in one hand, a long knife in the other. Once inside the tunnel, the men moved quickly.

"They can't be far ahead," Hoffmann whispered, as he led the fast-moving group. Rapidly they covered the distance that the teens had traversed, until they came to the crossing. Here Hoffmann stopped and flashed his light to the left and right.

"Which way?" he asked quietly.

"Be quiet and listen," said Kala. "Perhaps we will hear them and learn which path they took."

The men stood silently, listening. Long moments passed.

"I heard something to the left," Kala said quietly.

"I didn't," Walther said. He didn't trust Kala and he never had. Like most men who fight with their fists, Walther despised a knife-fighter, and Kala had a fearsome reputation with the blade.

Hoffmann stood a moment in thought. Then he made up his mind. "Walther, you and Stefan go straight ahead. Kala and I will make a quick trip to the left to check that sound. We'll rejoin you if we don't find anyone."

Quickly Hoffmann stepped off to the left, with Kala right behind him.

Walther was angered that Hoffmann had accepted Kala's advice. Then he controlled himself. "Let's go" he snapped to Stefan, and moved rapidly ahead on their original path. Both men had their lights in their hands. But within thirty feet, they found another passage. This also came in from the left. They stopped, puzzled.

"Which way now?" Stefan asked quietly. More and more he had to fight down the growing panic that came on him when he was underground. He hated narrow spaces. It was cool in the tunnel, yet his clothes were wet with the sweat that came from fear. But he was determined that Walther and the others would never know this. *When we catch those people and dispose of them, then we'll get back to that treasure and I'll be the first one out with some loot. I've got to get out of here!*

"I say we go straight ahead," Walter said after a moment. He led off at a fast pace, and Stefan followed.

"THE WALL'S FALLING IN!"

"The steps end right here," David whispered.

Slowly, carefully, he stepped down to the level floor, and made room for the others to join him. They faced a blank stone wall. To the right was a narrow door. David moved closer and studied this with his light.

"Just a wooden door," he said. Gripping the heavy iron ring that protruded from the door, he gave it a turn and shoved. To David's surprise, the door moved easily in his hand, swinging as if on oiled hinges. Peering inside, David let out his breath.

"Wow," he said

The others crowded around him and gasped. The beams of their flashlights illumined a room full of gold. Gold shields, gold masks, tall gold vessels set on the floor, and, at the far end of the room, a long gold altar with strangely designed gold vessels set on it.

"Boy," Mark said in quiet awe, "Look at that."

Slowly the four walked into the room, flashing their lights to left and right. All along the length of the wall to their left were rows and rows of gold shields, from the floor to the ceiling. And on the opposite wall, to their right, were rows of spears with sharp gold tips. These protruded into the room, reflecting the beams from their flashlights with startling brilliance.

"Look at those spears!" Penny said, amazed.

"There must be a hundred of them," Maria said. "They cover the whole wall."

"To match those shields across the room," Mark suggested. "They look like they've got gold tips, but I bet there's iron under that gold."

Hesitantly, the four walked farther into the narrow room. The rows of gold shields on the left, and the banks of gold-tipped spears on the right, gave them all a sense of fabulous wealth - and great danger.

"How many treasure rooms does this place have?" David asked, sweeping his light around the walls.

But Penny asked a question of her own before anyone could answer David. "What's that on that altar?" Taking her camera out of her case, she began to walk toward the low gold-covered structure with strange-looking gold vessels sitting on its top.

Before anyone could reply to Penny's question, Maria looked at the wall of shields to her left, and asked a question of her own. "Look, there's a door between two of those shields! Where does that go?"

David had a sudden sense that they were all becoming confused in this room. No one was answering the questions of the other - instead, each was going off in a different direction.

What's happening to us? he wondered. *We're all getting distracted!*

Maria walked over to the door in the wall to their left and stopped. Protruding from the heavy door was a gold knob. The Spanish girl hesitated a moment and glanced back at Mark. Then she twisted the knob and gave it a push. The door swung open at once, as easily as the one David had opened to let them into this room. Mark saw this and came to join her.

"Wonder what's inside?" he asked, intrigued. Forgetting their agreement to stick together, Mark stepped past her and walked through the narrow opening. Maria came after him, flashing her light around the room. Both gasped in amazement. This room too was filled with gold objects; vases on the floor and shields interspersed with strange idols set in the walls. As Maria swept the beam of her light around, their eyes were dazzled by the brilliantly shining gold-covered treasures.

"Look at those," Mark said quietly.

"And look, Mark, there's a door in the opposite wall! Isn't that the direction to the other side of the temple? To the outside?"

She couldn't keep the excitement out of her voice.

"I think it is," he replied. But his attention was on the gold shields on the wall to their right.

"Look at those designs," he said, beginning to walk toward them. "Hey, here's another door, where the far wall joins this one we just came through. Wonder where that leads?"

"This seems almost magical," Maria exclaimed. "See how the light flashes off all the gold."

In the room Mark and Maria had just left, Penny was taking pictures of the shields on the wall. Then she turned to David, her face shining with excitement. "This is incredible."

"Sure is," he agreed, grinning at her enthusiasm. Looking at her happy face, he began to forget the sense of unease that had been growing on him. I guess *we've got a few moments to study these treasures,* he thought.

"I'm going to photograph the walls," she said. "I'll be fast. Shine your light on those gold shields, will you? I don't want to use my flash."

She stepped into the middle of the room and began to frame her shots. Then she walked over to the wall for a close-up of the shields, while David played the beams of his light on them. Soon she was lost in the enthralling project.

"These are fabulous, David," she exclaimed. "Turn your light upward a bit." Completely forgetting Hoffmann and his men, she asked David to aim at different parts of the wall as she took picture after picture.

Then she turned to the other wall, and walked toward it. "Now shine your light on those gold-tipped spears," she said. "I'll take a shot from right under them!" Walking close to the spears, she took several pictures of the beautiful deadly weapons.

"Look," she said suddenly, "the spears in the upper rows are longer than those below them. They seem to taper and get shorter as they approach the floor. I wonder why?"

David angled his light downward and saw that the spears were indeed shorter in the rows that were nearer to the floor. *That's curious,* he thought. Stepping back a few feet, he pondered this, as Penny continued to take pictures.

"I can't imagine why those spears in the top rows are so much longer than those at the bottom!" she remarked again. "It's almost as if they're shaved downward! There must be a reason!"

David wondered why this had gotten her attention; she'd mentioned it twice, now. Then he had a sudden suspicion that there was a reason—a deadly reason. He was about to mention this, but Penny spoke first.

"Now I'll photograph those gold vessels on the altar," she said. "Oh, David, I can't tell what they are, but they are so beautiful." She walked quickly toward the steps that led up to the altar.

Suddenly, David had a premonition of terrible danger.

"Penny, Wait!"

He spoke too late.

The instant Penny set her foot on the first step leading to the altar, a loud *crack* came from the wall of spears to their right - she had stepped on another trap!

Penny cried out in alarm, and whirled around, her eyes darting to the rows of spears—the wall that held them was falling into the room!

"The wall's crashing!" she cried.

Terrible cracking sounds struck their ears as the wall of spears came falling toward them. The deadly long gold points would cover every square foot of the floor.

David lunged desperately toward Penny.

Some distance away from the crashing wall of stone with its scores of gold-headed spears, Hoffmann and Kala halted in shock.

"What was that?" Hoffmann exclaimed.

"Part of the building fell," Kala said, gripping his knife. "That's the sound of stone falling on stone." The two men stood puzzled at the dreadful sounds of crashing stones, feeling through their feet the tremors in the floor.

"Those people ahead of us must have knocked over something," Hoffmann said.

"It was too loud for anything people could knock over," Kala said. "That was a ceiling falling in, or a wall."

"Then they walked into a trap," Hoffmann guessed. "We were warned to watch for traps!"

"They weren't," Kala said grimly. "Whoever they are—or were—I don't think they'll trouble us anymore."

Hoffmann stood for a moment in silence. Then he agreed. "I think you are right." He smiled a wicked smile. "Let's go back and get the others—we've got a treasure to steal."

"Excellent," Kala agreed, his dark face breaking into a grin, his teeth flashing. "I'm ready for that."

The men turned and began to climb back up the steps.

They stopped in their tracks when they heard a girl scream.

SEPARATED

David leaped toward Penny, grabbed her in his arms, and brought her stumbling around the left side of the altar as the wall fell toward them from their right. Then he dropped to his knees, bringing her down with him, and held her against the side of the wide stone structure as the wall collapsed inward and smashed into the room.

A row of gold-tipped spears flashed over the edge of the altar just above their heads, struck sparks as they crashed into the floor, and shattered. Stones from the falling wall fell in front of, behind, and on top of the altar, just missing the two teens that cowered fearfully close beside it. The successive rows of spears struck sparks as they too hit the stone floor and shattered; flying wood and rock went everywhere.

Their ears were stunned with the dreadful sounds of the crashing stone falling on stone. But the wall had fallen in from their right, and by crouching against the left side of the altar they had been protected both from the angled spears and from the falling wall. They were shaken, but unhurt.

David glanced at the back wall of the room just a few feet from where he crouched; he still held Penny in his arms. Stones and shattered spears met his eyes. He darted a look toward the wall that held the gold shields. There was a jumble of wreckage several feet deep against that wall, blocking half of the door through which Mark and Maria had just passed. Two whole rows of the gold shields had been knocked to the floor and were buried under the fallen stone.

"Quick," David said suddenly. "We've got to get out of here before the ceiling falls down." He jumped to his feet, and pulled her up to stand beside him.

"Where can we go?" she asked.

"Look, in the corner where the falling wall hit the back wall. There's the door we saw a moment ago. We've got to climb over those rocks and go through that."

David whirled around and shouted toward the door through which Mark and Maria had gone, now half-blocked by fallen stones. "Mark, come back here—we've found a door. Hurry."

"We're coming," Mark yelled.

David grabbed Penny's hand and helped her scramble over the jumble of broken stones and spears toward the door behind the altar.

Suddenly Maria screamed.

Through the doorway David and Penny heard Mark shout, "Get back, Maria!" Then his voice was drowned by the sound of crashing stone from within that room too. David and Penny whirled around on the treacherous footing of broken stone and looked toward the doorway: it was now almost closed by broken stones!

"Mark, Maria, are you all right?" Penny called desperately.

There was no answer.

"It's blocked, David; their door is blocked," Penny cried.

"Mark," David called. But then he felt the pile of broken rock beneath their feet begin to tremble.

"Quick, Penny," he said, "this floor's shaking. Get back."

Frantically they turned and scrambled back over the pile of stones toward the base of the altar. The floor was giving way beneath the weight of the fallen wall.

"Mark." David called again.

"David, how can they get back here?" Penny cried. "Was that part of the same trap that fell on us?"

Suddenly they heard Mark's strong voice through the narrow opening.

"David, I heard you. We're okay. We're safe in a doorway that leads out of here. We'll keep heading toward the opposite side of the temple and meet you outside…"

But his voice was cut off by the crashing of more falling rock. Now the door between the two treasure rooms was blocked. David and Penny heard his voice no more.

"Mark," Penny cried in anguish.

"Quick, Penny," David said, gripping her hand. "They're all right, He said he'd meet us outside. We'll keep working our way to that side of the temple. We've got to go through this near door and get out of this room right away."

But the floor between the altar and the narrow door was jammed with broken spears and broken stones, and it was not easy for David and Penny to climb through.

"Watch out that you don't break your ankle," David warned, as, hand in hand, steadying each other, they stepped gingerly through the wreckage, guided by the beams of their flashlights.

Then David saw a spear sticking out of the pile of wreckage. He put his light in his pocket, and yanked the spear out of the jumbled stones. Broken by the collapse of the wall, it was only five feet long—but the long gleaming gold point was intact.

He felt the point. "This is sharp," he exclaimed. *Maybe this will come in handy,* he thought to himself as he gripped the thick wooden handle.

"Oh, David," Penny said. "I'm praying they're all right."

"Me too. I think this whole place is connected with traps to protect the treasures. But we've got to get out of this room. Then we can work our way to that side of the temple. That's what they're doing, so we'll meet them outside. Then we'll run for the plane and fly home."

They came to the door in the back of the wrecked room. David released Penny's hand, and pulled out his flashlight.

"Careful," he warned.

He stepped gingerly over the rocks, ducked his head, and pushed on a golden knob. The door creaked, but swung open; David looked into a tunnel. In the strong beam of his light he could see that it went straight ahead, and that within a dozen yards there were also passages leading off to both sides.

Dropping the spear, he gripped her hand and helped her into the tunnel entrance. Then he reached back and picked up the spear.

"Let's go," he said. "We've got to get out of here before anything else falls."

Hurriedly David led her through the tunnel, the spear in one hand, the flashlight in the other. They came at once to an intersection—another tunnel crossed at right angles. The two stopped, and flashed their lights to right and left.

"The passage to the right goes on a long way," he said, seeing no end in the beam of his flashlight.

"So does the one in front," Penny said. "But the one to the left turns back left again. That would take us to the room we just got out of. Or the one next to it—the one Mark and Maria went in. And those rooms are wrecked. Don't you think we should go straight ahead?"

"Yes," he agreed. "Let's go." Their voices sounded strangely hollow as they reverberated in the stone passage.

Before they could move they were suddenly illuminated by the powerful beam of a light that shone on them from the right-hand passage! They heard an all-too familiar voice shout, "Halt!"

"Hoffmann!" Penny said, in horror.

"WE'VE GOT THEM NOW!"

Far behind David and Penny, standing in the doorway opposite the one through which they'd entered the room, Mark and Maria faced terrible danger. The narrow beams of their flashlights pierced the over-powering darkness that surrounded them, but did nothing to lighten the feeling of doom.

"Quick, Maria," Mark said, "We've got to get out of here before any more of the ceiling falls in."

Mark released her hand and grabbed the thick gold knob of the wooden door.

"Be careful," Maria said, fearful suddenly of another trap.

Slowly he eased the door open. It too moved as if on silent hinges. Stepping quickly inside, he flashed his light around.

"Another treasure room," he said.

Maria came swiftly through the door and stood beside him. "It's just like the other," she said, sweeping the beam of her light around the walls.

"There's another door across from us." Mark said. "That's the direction we want—hurry."

"Watch out for traps on the floor," she warned, as they headed for the door that was illumined by their lights.

Mark shone the light on the floor before him, and then swept it around to the left and right.

"The stones all look the same," he said, "and there's nothing else we can do—we've got to keep going."

They rushed across the room and stopped before the door.

"I don't like that door, Mark," she said suddenly, in a tense voice. She was clearly afraid.

"Why not?" They stood close together in a sea of darkness.

"I don't know; this one just gives me a feeling of terrible danger! Please, Mark, let's go through that other one." She aimed her light at the door to their right, at the far wall. "Maybe we'll meet Penny and David quicker that way."

He stood for a moment in indecision. Then he made up his mind. "But I think we want to head back in this direction as soon as we can."

"I think so too," she said. "But I'm afraid of this door!"

"Then don't be—we won't go through it. We'll take that far door, see if we can't meet them, then we'll all turn back toward the other side of the temple and get out of this place."

FLIGHT FROM THE TEMPLE

They hurried across the room to the smaller door and stopped before this for a moment. This door too had a gold knob. Mark grabbed and twisted the knob, and pushed the door slowly open. He shone his light inside.

"Another tunnel," he said quietly. "I can't see the end." He hesitated for a moment, wondering what to do. But they had no choice, he realized, but to go on.

"C'mon," he said confidently. "We'll get out of here as fast as we can and meet Penny and David outside."

"Do you think they got away?" she asked.

"Sure I do," he said firmly. "David said they were heading for a door in the far wall. So they're going the same way we are, like you thought. We'll probably meet them ahead."

In another part of the temple, Walther and Stefan had felt—and heard—the dreadful sounds of the falling rock wall. The two stopped in their tracks.

"What's that?" Stefan asked, alarmed, fighting back his growing terror with difficulty.

"Quick," Walther replied, turning around and breaking into a run. "Things are falling apart. We've got to find Hoffmann and Kala."

Stefan ran after him, to the place where the four men had parted. Then they turned down the passageway Hoffmann and Kala had taken, and continued running until they joined Hoffmann and Kala who were running toward them.

"This way," Hoffmann yelled. "We've heard those people! A girl screamed! Now we've got them," He turned and raced down the passage, with Kala close behind. Walther and Stefan raced after them.

We're going deeper and deeper into this temple, Stefan thought. He was on the verge of panic now. *I've got to get out!*

Struggling with his rising fear, Stefan failed to see the big man ahead of him stumble, then recover. Walther had almost tripped in a depression in the stone floor, but he regained his balance, and kept running. Stefan's foot hit this same dip in the floor, he lost his balance, plunged forward, pumped his legs desperately to keep from falling—and crashed into Walther's back.

Walther was knocked sprawling onto the stone floor, smashing his nose. Cursing in anger and pain he threw off Stefan and scrambled to his feet. Bellowing with rage, the big man wiped his sleeve across his bloody face, and drew back his fist to strike the cowering pilot.

Ahead of them, Hoffmann had found David and Penny! "Halt!" he cried, as he flashed his light down a passage to the left and saw two figures just forty yards away, transfixed in the powerful beam. He recognized them at once.

They raced across the intersection of the passages, and out of his sight.

"It's those kids," Hoffmann screamed uncontrollably. "Those kids that ruined my plans this summer. I've got them."

Filled with fury, he dashed down the passage toward the intersection. Kala ran behind him. Neither noticed that Walther and Stefan were not following.

David and Penny ran down the narrow passage way and came to another intersection, where a wider passage crossed their own at right angles.

David skidded to a stop, and said, "Left, Penny, you go ahead. Fast."

Penny turned and raced down the passage, flashing her light ahead to illumine the way, with David close behind. The narrow tunnel widened suddenly, by a couple of feet to each side, and David realized at once that if they backed up against the wall, their pursuers would not be able to see them with their flashlights from the intersection.

"Stop, Penny," David whispered. "Turn off your light. Get against the wall. They won't be able to see us when they reach that that crossing back there! Press yourself against the wall, but keep moving."

Behind them, Hoffmann and Kala came to a sudden stop at the intersection.

"Which way did they go?" Hoffmann yelled in rage, as he shone his light to left and right, searching for his prey. Kala did the same.

The beam flashed past David and Penny, who were hidden from view by the widened tunnel. The two teens, backs pressed against the wall, continued to move silently down the passage.

"I can't see where they've gone!" Hoffmann snapped angrily. "They've just disappeared!"

Suddenly he heard Walther screaming, back in the passageway behind them. "What's that madman yelling about?" Hoffmann said suddenly, shocked that Walther and Stefan were not with them. "We need them here at once." He dashed back the way he'd come.

"Keep flashing your light down the tunnels, to see which way they went," he called to Kala as he ran to get Walther and Stefan.

Kala turned his light down the passageway ahead of him, then swept it to the left, and then to the right. He couldn't understand why his powerful light did not illumine their quarry—they were not in view straight ahead, nor to the left, nor to the right.

David and Penny, their backs pressed against the wall, continued to move sideways, just covered from Kala's light by the indentation of the wall. Their hearts raced faster when Kala's powerful beam swept past, illuminating the way ahead. Then the passage grew black as Kala turned his light in the other direction. Far away, they heard men shouting.

"Keep moving, Penny," David whispered. "Fast as you can and still be quiet. But keep your hand out ahead of your head so you don't hit anything. And stay against the wall!"

In complete darkness—except when Kala's beam flashed down the passage—David and Penny moved sideways against the wall. Penny kept her left hand at the level of her head, feeling her way carefully as she moved. David did the same.

"This is slow going," David whispered reassuringly. "But they can't see us, and they don't know which passage we took. And we're moving farther away!"

The sounds of distant arguing men came down the dark passage. David and Penny had no way of knowing that Stefan was backing away in panic from the huge Walther, who pursued him with murderous threats, while Hoffmann was yelling for them to join him.

"Join us, Walther!" Hoffmann yelled in fury, as he ran back down the passageway toward the two. "We've got to catch those kids!" Now he could see Walther's back in his light.

Walther finally stopped and turned to Hoffmann, who blinded him with his flashlight.

"What are you men yelling about, Walther?" Hoffmann demanded. "We've found them!"

"This clumsy fool knocked me down and broke my nose!" Walther yelled, as he turned again to pursue Stefan.

"I didn't mean too!" Stefan yelled, "I tripped!"

"You're the fool, Walther!" Hoffmann yelled. "You're the fool! There's a treasure waiting for us! Come back and help me catch those kids! Then we'll get that gold. The gold, Walther!"

At the sound of *gold* the enraged Walther halted his pursuit of Stefan. Slowly he turned.

"I didn't mean to run into you!" Stefan yelled again. "I tripped!"

"All right," Walther said disgustedly. "But stay out of my way!" He wiped his sleeve across his broken nose again, and turned to follow Hoffmann.

Far from Hoffmann now, Kala stood at the intersection, shining his light continuously down the left-hand passage, then straight ahead, and then down the right-hand passage, hoping to spot anyone who moved. David and Penny, their backs pressed against the wall, were getting farther and farther away from him, but he didn't know it. Quietly, but steadily, they moved to increase their distance from their pursuers. Suddenly Penny came to a halt. Her heart beat madly.

"David, there's a door blocking the way!" she whispered.

"Back up, and let me by," he said at once.

She moved back toward him. He glanced behind, saw the dim beam of Kala's light far down the hall, saw it pass, and pressed quickly by her.

He felt the door at once, and his hands groped frantically across its surface until his hand found a knob. "Pray that it opens!" Slowly he pressed against the door as he twisted the knob.

The door didn't budge.

"IT GOES STRAIGHT DOWN!"

"We've been going forever!" Maria whispered, as she followed Mark in the blackness of the narrow passage.

"It sure seems like it," he agreed. Then he stopped suddenly. "The tunnel ends!" he said somberly, as his light shone on a wall ahead. He flashed the beam on the wall and ceiling and floor. *Are we trapped in a dead end?* he asked himself, fighting against fear.

"Is there a door?" she asked.

"No, but look. There's a trap door in the floor." Mark knelt quickly to inspect it.

She came up and knelt beside him. Together they studied the trap door. A thick round iron handle was fastened to the wood. Through this handle an iron bar passed, and extended to another iron loop imbedded in the floor. The door was thus locked so it could not be unlocked and opened from below - unless someone in the passage first removed the iron bar.

"Is there no other way out?" she asked, shining her light above her. But the stone walls and the ceiling showed no evidence of another opening.

"This is it," Mark said bleakly. He sighed. Then he set his light on the floor, and pulled out the iron bar locking shut the door. This was hard to do, but finally he got it out. Then he pulled on the handle of the trap door.

It didn't budge.

He looked at Maria with a sinking heart, hoping that she couldn't see the anxiety on his face. Then he stood up, straddled the trap door with his feet, grabbed the iron handle, and tugged with all his strength. Slowly, with a hideous screech, the door came open, swinging reluctantly and noisily on rusted hinges. Mark opened it all the way and bent it back till it lay on the floor.

The two knelt shoulder to shoulder in the narrow place and shone their lights downward. Below them, a ladder bolted to the stone wall led straight down. They aimed their lights to search for the bottom, but the darkness seemed to swallow the beams in a strange way, and they could not make out what was at the bottom of this vertical tunnel.

"Mark, I hear rushing water! Could that be the stream that we saw from the plane, the stream that runs under the temple?" she asked excitedly.

"Could be," he said thoughtfully, as he peered into the depths and tried to figure out what was at the end of their lights. "But I can't be sure."

"The passage goes straight down," she said in a frightened voice.

Her words seemed to hang in the air—Mark didn't know what to say.

"But we can't do anything else, can we," she continued quietly. "We can't go back. There's no other way for us to go but down."

"I'm afraid so," Mark said. He didn't like this at all. "Can you climb down that ladder?"

"Sure," she said, "if it's not too far. But we don't know what we'll find at the bottom, do we?"

"No, we don't." Mark was bitterly disappointed; he'd hoped they'd have more choices than this. *I was sure we'd find passages going left,* he thought to himself, *passages that would lead us to the other side of the temple. But not this!*

"Well," he said, "if it's really the stream that we saw from the air, maybe it takes us out from under the temple. Why else would this ladder be here?" He hoped this was true. "I'll go down first," he continued. "We'll go slow."

"Let's pray first, Maria," he said. Mark prayed, thanking the Lord for all His goodness to them, for all His protection, for forgiveness; then he asked the Lord to guide them safely out of the temple, and to lead Penny and David safely out too. Maria prayed then, and repeated the request for Penny and David.

"Remember, Maria," he said earnestly, "Climbing down this ladder will be no problem for me. But if it gets hard for you to hold on, tell me right away. I'll come back up, stand behind you, and you can lean against me and rest your arms. Okay?"

"Okay," she said.

"We'd better get rid of our packs," he added. "We don't need extra weight going down that ladder. Let's drop 'em down so we'll have them when we get down."

They slipped off their packs, then dropped them down, but barely heard the sound of their landing. Then Mark turned off his light, stuck it in his pocket, set his feet on the iron rungs, and began to descend, facing the wall as he climbed down. Maria looked carefully to see just where she was going to put her feet. Then she too turned off her light and put it into her pocket. She groped for the rungs, found these, climbed over the edge, and began to follow Mark down the ladder. Now they were in absolute darkness.

"Stop, Maria," Mark said suddenly. I'm going to turn my light back on and hook it to my belt so I can see what's below."

Mark held to the ladder with one hand, pulled his flashlight from his trouser pocket with the other, turned it on, and fumbled around on his belt until he found a loop. He attached the hook on the light to this and it lit their way below.

"Now I can at least see where we're going," he said, trying to be cheerful. "Let's go."

"This is scary, Mark," Maria whispered, as she climbed slowly, carefully, after him.

"It sure is," he agreed. "We're getting there, though."

For several minutes they descended quietly in the blackness. Then Maria spoke. "I think the dark is worse than the climbing."

"So do I. Time for me to stop and look down—don't step on me." He stopped his descent, and looked below. The light shone on the dark vertical tunnel, but he still could not be sure what was on the bottom below.

"What can you see?" she asked eagerly. Her arms were feeling the strain of this unaccustomed climbing now.

"I just can't be sure," he said hesitantly.

"But I can hear the sound of water," she said.

"Me, too. But I just can't be sure if that's what I'm seeing. Let's keep going, then we'll look again. I don't want you to have to hold on longer than you have to."

They continued their descent.

"It's damp," she noticed. The iron rungs were slippery under her hands and feet, and sometimes her shoes slipped. "Don't go too fast!" Her arms were tiring.

"I won't," he said.

Then Mark realized that he should give Maria a rest.

"Let's stop and rest a minute," he said. "Come closer, then stop and get close to the ladder. I'll come up behind you, and you can lean on me and rest your arms. This tunnel is narrow, and I'll be able to lean against the wall."

Maria descended a few more rungs, and then stopped. Marked climbed up behind her and leaned back against the wall. "Relax your arms," he said, "and lean on me."

"Are you sure you can lean on the wall?" she asked.

"Sure am."

She relaxed her arms, barely holding on to the cold damp iron rungs, and let her back årest against his chest. His arms were around her, gripping the ladder. Her arms trembled when she released the rungs. Gradually, she relaxed.

"I'm not so afraid now," she said.

"Good!" he replied. "Rest as long as you need, 'cause I'm resting against the wall. When you're ready, we'll start again." But he kept his grip on the ladder with both hands, not taking a chance of slipping and causing them both to fall.

For a short while he held her like this while she rested against him. Then she said, "I'm fine now. Thanks."

"Great," he said. "You're brave, Maria. We'll reach the bottom soon. But tell me if you get tired again, and we'll rest. First let me take another look below."

Mark leaned to the side and looked along the beam of the light hooked to his belt. This time he was sure the light was shining on sand.

"Wow!" he said. "That sure does sound like moving water. And I can see sand. And I see something else—I think it's the prow of a boat."

"A boat!"

"Looks like it." he said. "Let's go, we're at the end!"

"Oh, Mark, do you think we can get out of the temple?"

"You bet we can!" he said.

"But what will David and Penny do?" she asked suddenly, remembering that they too were lost in this strange stone building.

"I'm sure there have got to be ways out of the temple just like the way we came in," he said. "They can follow the tunnels just like we did, and they'll probably find one that lets them out the side wall. We'll meet them outside."

Their spirits soared as they descended the next few feet. Mark glanced down again, and couldn't keep the excitement out of his voice. "We're close to the end. The tunnel gets wider now!"

Now they were almost at the bottom of the ladder. Mark crouched on the rung, leaned downward as far as he could, and searched the space below with his light. "There's the stream."

"Oh, Mark, we made it!"

In another moment the two were standing together on the bank beside the rushing stream.

"You're mighty brave, Maria," he said, holding her until her arms stopped trembling.

"Look!" he said, releasing her and shining his light around them. Four dugout canoes were on the bank, their prows just at the edge of the fast-moving stream. Two rows of large jars were stacked neatly against the wall of the temple. A row of broad-bladed paddles stood behind the jars, and beside these was a row of tall spears.

"Watch out for snakes, Mark," Maria warned suddenly, as Mark walked over toward the paddles.

"You bet I will," he replied, flashing his light on the ground as he walked. He picked up two paddles, and brought these back to the edge of the water. Then he went back and took down two of the long iron-tipped spears; he had suddenly remembered the wild pigs that had rushed to the entrance just after they had entered the temple.

"Man, these are fighting weapons, all right. And, Maria, these canoes don't look so old. I think natives have been using this place to fish and store boats and supplies, and not so long ago."

"But they couldn't have opened that trap door we came through, could they?" she asked. "You had to unbolt it in the tunnel."

"That's right. That's why no one could have gotten into the tunnel from here all these years. But let's us get out of this place."

"Mark," Maria said, as she knelt on the bank and prepared to get in the canoe. "Look downstream." She pointed to her left, in the direction the water was rushing.

"What do you see?" he asked quickly, rushing to her side.

"I can see light."

He knelt beside her and looked down the tunnel through which the stream was moving. She was right.

"Let's go," he said. He put the paddles and spears in the canoe. "Have you ever paddled one of these?" he asked suddenly.

"Oh, yes," she exclaimed.

"Great. But I'll paddle first while you shine your light ahead so we can see where we're going. I'll put the boat in the water and hold it while you get in. There are no seats, so kneel in the front and stay low."

He shoved one of the paddles forward, and then put the canoe in the water. Maria climbed in from the low bank. Mark got in after her, turned off his light, and shoved off. At once the boat began to move with the flowing steam. Maria took out her flashlight, switched it on, and aimed it downstream. Mark began to paddle gently—then stopped. The stream itself was moving them as fast as he wanted to go and all he had to do was steer.

Oh Lord, he thought, *don't let anything block our way out of here!*

He didn't mention this fear to Maria.

"QUICK, PENNY! GET INSIDE!"

Back in the temple, in the darkened passage, Penny held her breath as David shoved with his shoulder against the door. Far down the tunnel to her right, Kala's light swept by periodically, but the beam no longer reached them.

"The door's stuck," he whispered hoarsely. Again he shoved.

The door moved an inch. David pushed again, hard as he could.

Finally the door began to open under the pressure of David's strength and then it stopped. He shoved again with all his power, and a terrible screech rang out from the protesting hinges and reverberated down the passage as the door swung wide open.

"Quick, Penny," he said, his heart racing. "Get inside. They'll hear that for sure, and come after us in a hurry."

She dashed into the room, with David right behind. David pressed the door shut, switched on his light, turned and aimed the beam on the door as he searched frantically for a bolt. There was none. *How can I block this door so those men can't open it and catch us?* he asked himself frantically.

Whirling, he turned and swept the light around the room. Rows and rows of tall clay jars, many four and five feet high, stood on the floor and on shelves against the walls. These were black, with strange red figures painted on them.

"Can I get one of those to the door before they come?" he asked, rushing toward the jars. Suddenly he tripped on something, and then quickly regained his balance. Flashing his light to the floor, he saw a pair of grooves, like tracks, cut in the stone. These led to the walls on either side of the door, above which rows of shelves rose, each laden with the big jars. Sweeping his light along the floor by the walls, he saw other tracks.

"These must be tracks for dollies or something, to take those heavy jars to the shelves."

"I've got it," he said exultantly. He jammed the broken shaft of the spear he carried in one of the grooves in the floor, and then pressed the iron point against the door, under the knob. Then he had another idea: drawing his knife from its sheath, he jammed that under the door as well.

"Maybe that'll keep them out while we get away," he said. "Now let's find a way out of here."

"There's a door in each wall, and one is huge," Penny said. "Which one shall we take?"

FLIGHT FROM THE TEMPLE

They swept their lights around the room. Directly across from where they stood was a door just like the one through which they'd entered. To the right was a large entrance, high, with double doors. And in the wall to their left was a smaller door like the one across the hall.

"I think that's the way we want to go," he said quickly, pointing to the smaller door.

"I do too," she replied. "I think that's the way to the side of the temple—the side opposite to the one we first came in! I *think* that's right, David."

"So do I," he agreed. "Anyway, it leads us directly away from those men—let's go."

They rushed across the hall. David pushed open the door and their lights shone on another narrow passage.

Then Penny had an idea. "What do you think about opening one of those other doors? Maybe that would make them think we went that way?"

"Good idea," he said. Dashing to his left he pushed open the door, and then brought it back until it was almost closed. "Don't want to make it too obvious," he said, and ran back to Penny.

Suddenly there was a crashing against the door across the room; the one through which they'd entered a moment before.

"They're here already," she said in alarm.

"C'mon. Go through and I'll close this."

She went through the door; David followed, and then pulled the door shut. He flashed his light on the wood, but saw no bolt with which he could lock it behind them. Nor was there anything in the tunnel to prop against the door.

"Let's go," he said, deeply disappointed, but making no comment to Penny: he just hoped the spear and the knife blade would jam the other door so their pursuers couldn't get in. Shining his light ahead, he began to trot down the passage. She was right behind him.

"Watch your head," she warned suddenly.

"Thanks!" he replied, remembering to flash his light upward as well as before him.

Then the passage widened, and before him appeared a sinister sight. David slowed, and came to a stop.

"What is it?" she said at once, coming up behind him.

"Look at that." He shone his light on a fierce-looking crocodile-headed statue standing in a wide passage before them. They could see that the passage continued on behind the statue. Behind the statue, they could see a flight of stairs leading upwards.

"That's awful," she said with a shudder.

"Just like the others we saw back there," he replied.

"Just like the statues in Pharaoh's tomb," she reminded him.

"Let's go," he said quickly. They ran past the statue and toward the flight of steps leading to the next level.

"Boy," David said. "We want to go *down*, not *up*, but there's no other way."

"Yet this is heading the way we want," she pointed out.

"Yeah, I think it is. C'mon."

This passage too was wider. Side by side they went up the stairs, shining their lights ahead as they ascended. Reaching the next level, they flashed their lights on the stones before the door, then stepped into a broad room.

"There's a door on the other side," she said.

But are there traps in the floor? David wondered, as they started to cross the room.

"Let's be careful, Penny," he said. "We don't want to stumble into a trap now!"

They studied the floor before them, searching for any sign that might reveal a trap. But they saw nothing to cause them to stop, so they pressed deeper into the room.

Will we ever find our way out of here? Penny wondered.

A few minutes later, their passage ended at yet another door. This one opened easily, however.

What they faced now struck them with dread.

Black darkness greeted them. Flashing their lights ahead, they saw to their horror that they stood before a small stone platform, a platform jutting out from the doorway, seeming to hang in the darkness above a deep abyss that gaped beyond and below them. The floor just came to an end. On the vertical wall to their right was a narrow ledge, apparently a footpath leading from the doorway in which they stood, out into the darkness. Flashing their lights along this ledge they saw at its end another vertical wall of stone, directly across from them, with its own small stone platform jutting into the air toward them, connected to the narrow ledge. Behind this they saw the faint outline of a door.

David guessed that the distance from where they stood, to the platform, and the door on the other side, was more than forty yards.

From the darkness below they heard the sound of rushing waters.

The dugout canoe shot out from under the low stone tunnel into the brightness of the unclouded sun. Involuntarily, both Mark and Maria shut their eyes for a moment. "We're out, Mark!" she cried.

They both looked back at the towering bulk of the temple mound behind and above them.

"We want to get out on the right-hand bank," he said at once, blinking as his eyes adjusted to the unaccustomed brilliance. "Penny and David are heading the same way we did, and they'll come out on this side. We'll hide behind those bushes and watch for them. Then we'll go for the plane."

Neither voiced to the other the fear that Penny and David might not come out of the temple.

The huge mass of the vine-covered temple mound towered ominously behind them as Mark steered the canoe to the low bank on their right. From the water's edge the ground was covered with short grass until it reached the trees and underbrush beyond.

The two scrambled out of the canoe, Mark hauled the craft up on the grass, and then laid the paddles beside it. Taking the two spears out of the boat, he handed one to Maria.

"What in the world will I do with this?" she asked.

"I don't know," he replied honestly, "but it's a weapon if we need one. Let's hold on to them." He didn't tell her about the wild pigs. They turned and faced the jungle. He wondered how the two of them would stop half-a-dozen charging angry beasts.

"Oh Mark, I feared we'd never get out of that awful place," she said, smiling brightly as they hurried toward the trees.

"Me too," he said, grinning at her happy face. "But we did."

"How will we know where David and Penny will come out?" she asked.

"I don't know," he said. "That's the problem—I don't know. It could be anywhere along this side of the mound."

"Even if they find a door, they've got to work their way out through all those vines and underbrush that covers the temple, don't they?" she said.

"Yeah, they sure do. But if we see them I can climb up those vines and help. I think we should head toward the woods to our left, and watch the temple from behind some of those bushes. We can see anyone who comes out, but if Hoffmann's men come out first, they wouldn't see us."

"Do you think Hoffmann's men *will* come out here?" she asked, eyes wide.

"I don't know, Maria," he said, trying to hide the alarm he felt. "But we've run into that man all summer long—time after time. There's just no way of knowing. I *think* that David and Penny are ahead of them, so they should get out first—but we just can't take a chance."

Quickly the two moved back till they were opposite the huge mound, angling left as they headed for the bushes and tall trees just fifty yards from the vine-covered building. They came through a batch of tall vegetation and halted in surprise.

A small plane was parked under the tall trees, its engine facing the temple-mound.

"That must be Hoffmann's plane!" she said.

"It must be." Mark stood a moment, undecided, a frown of concentration on his broad face. Then he made up his mind. "Let's go look at it. We'll check it out, then get into those trees."

Quickly the two rushed up to the craft. "This is bigger than ours," she said.

"It sure is," he answered. They went quickly to the door on the passenger side of the aircraft. Mark put his foot in the rung below the door, stepped up, and looked inside. Then he pulled the door open and stuck his head in.

"It's a six-seater," he told her in a quiet voice. "But they've taken out the back two seats, and left a lot of room for cargo. They also left the key. They're not expecting anyone, that's for sure. But neither were we."

"Mark, I think those men came to steal the treasure from the temple."

"I think you're right," he agreed. "But, quick, let's get back to those bushes opposite the temple and hide."

As they hurried back to their hiding place, Mark wondered if he should have taken the key from the plane's cockpit. He'd thought of it—then changed his mind. *I don't know if we want to alert Hoffmann's gang that someone else has found them. They'll probably be going back and forth as they load the treasure, and when David and Penny come out we can take the key then and run to our own plane.*

But he realized how dangerous their situation was: what if David and Penny came out of the temple just when Hoffmann's men did?

"THERE'S NO OTHER WAY!"

Deep inside the temple, David and Penny faced their dreadful choice.

"There's no other way?" she asked. Her voice trembled.

"Either we go back—toward those men—or we cross on that ledge. There's no other way," David replied somberly. He tried to keep his voice calm, but it wasn't easy.

"It's narrow, David," she said.

"It sure is," he replied.

David couldn't control the dreadful pounding of his heart at the terrifying prospect before them. They stood inside the doorway through which they'd just come. They'd rushed across the room with the greatest hopes, and now…

"Penny, to get across, we've got to walk along that ledge," he said grimly. "We've got to lean as close to the wall as we can."

The vertical dark stone wall gleamed menacingly in the beam of their flashlights.

"I hate heights, David," she said, tremulously.

"So do I," David's heart was pounding at the prospect before them. The ledge was just barely wide enough for them to stand on if they pressed themselves against the wall. They'd have to inch their way across, one step at a time, not daring to lean away from the wall even for a moment.

"Let's pray, Penny," he said. He put his arm around her shoulder and held her close. Then they both prayed.

"Can we keep our packs?" she wondered.

"No, we don't need any weight on our backs, pulling us backward. We'll have to leave them. But use the clip on your canteen to put it on your belt. We've got to keep our water."

"What about my camera?"

"Give it to me. I'll sling it around my neck." She handed him the camera.

"How far is it across to the other side?" she asked.

He flashed his beam across the deadly abyss. "I'd say forty yards," he said finally. "Here's what we'll do. We'll go slow, real slow. Put your flashlight in your pocket, we'll save it. I'll use mine, just so we don't get disoriented in the dark. Face the wall, put your hands against it, shoulder high, lightly though—don't push. And lean against the wall as you move, close as you can. Take small steps sideways, one at a time."

He shone the light on the vertical wall they'd have to scrape against as they crossed. Then he looked back at her. Her face was faint in the reflected light.

"Oh, David—what if I fall?"

"You won't fall, Penny. But if you do, you won't fall alone. I'll jump right with you. I'll never leave you."

"You're courageous, Penny," he said solemnly. Then David faced the wall, gripped the light in his left hand with the beam aimed sideways across the abyss, and placed his hands shoulder high against the stone. The wall was cold. The wall was damp.

"It's slick," he told her. "Be careful! Lean against the wall as close as you can. Just follow me."

He shone the light at their feet so she could see the ledge, and waited for her to position herself beside him.

Then he raised his left hand shoulder high so that the light shone once more across the abyss. Penny could see his body against the light.

"It helps to see you, David," she said.

"Good," he replied. He tried to think of something to say, something that might lighten the tension and make her smile for a moment. But nothing came to mind. Finally, all he could think of was, "Ready?"

"Ready."

David moved his left foot along the ledge, then his right. He did this again, moving one foot, and then the other. Now he had left the stone platform, his face was pressing the cold damp stone wall, his back was to the long fall to the waters below. He took another step.

"It works," he said. "Now you take a step." He waited.

Slowly she stepped out with her left foot, put her weight on this, and brought her right foot carefully onto the narrow ledge.

David stepped out again, then waited for her to do the same. Slowly, laboriously, covering less than a foot at a time, the two moved out along the perilously slender ledge, away from the stone platform that hung high in the darkness above the waters. David's light shone on the far wall, which seemed, he thought, to be a mile away.

"Close your eyes if you want," he said.

"It's better if I watch you," she answered.

"Okay, but just don't look down."

She didn't reply.

Small slow step by small slow step, farther and farther along the narrow ledge they moved. Soon they'd gone ten steps. Then twenty. Then thirty. David was counting to himself. *Forty yards is a hundred and twenty feet. We've taken thirty steps, and that's barely twenty feet. We've got a long way to go.*

Below them the noise of the waters suddenly increased. Violent splashing and grunting sounds rose from the depths.

"What's that, David?" Penny asked in alarm.

"I don't know!" he said, fighting to control his fear. "Don't pay any attention to what's below, Penny! Just concentrate on our goal. One step at a time. Just like everything in life, one step at a time."

"One step at a time," she repeated.

FLIGHT FROM THE TEMPLE

One small slow step at a time, Penny followed David along the precarious ledge into the darkness. Below them, the violent splashing and angry grunting sounds increased.

Those must be crocodiles! she thought wildly. *Crocodiles right below us. We can't fall!*

"Can you see?" he asked, to distract her, hoping some of his flashlight's beams directed at their destination would give her some encouragement—and also help her orientation, and her balance, on the perilously slender ledge.

"Enough," she said breathlessly. "David, those are awful sounds below us!"

"Don't listen," he said quickly. "Hum a tune. How about one of my favorites, 'City of New Orleans?'"

"I'll try," she said.

David began to hum, and she joined him. Humming feebly in the dreadful darkness, trying vainly to block from their minds the terrifying sounds that rose from crocodiles fighting to the death below them, the two continued their agonizing slow crossing on the wet stone ledge.

They were almost halfway across when Penny spoke again. David's heart froze at her words.

"My leg's starting to cramp, David!"

"THERE'S HOFFMANN!"

Hoffmann, Walther, and Stefan raced down the hall and pulled to a halt at the intersection of the passages where Kala waited. "I heard noise down that left-hand passage," Kala said quietly.

"Are you sure?" Walther asked, skeptically.

"Of course he's sure," Hoffmann snapped. "Let's go!"

Hoffmann aimed his beam down that passage and ran rapidly behind it. The others followed at once, and soon came to the widening in the tunnel.

"That's why we couldn't see them!" Kala said. "The tunnel is wider here and they could hide behind it and still move away from us. They were here all the time and I didn't know it!"

He was angry at himself for having been fooled.

"Well they can't hide now," Hoffmann said as he ran. "We've got them now." But he came to an abrupt halt at the door. Grabbing the knob, he shoved. The door didn't move. He shoved again. The others rushed up and halted behind him.

"Walther, help me open this door," Hoffmann snapped.

At once the big man threw his powerful body against the door. It shook, but didn't open.

"They've blocked it from inside," Kala said.

Hoffmann went berserk. "We can't let those kids get away!" he shouted. "They're going to pay for what they've done to me. I've got to get them!" He raged and cursed in the tunnel.

"Hoffmann," Kala said quietly. "The door is blocked. We must go back and get the treasure before they do."

Quietly, Kala reasoned with the man, as he'd reason to a distraught child.

Finally Hoffmann came to his senses. "You're right," he admitted. "We've got to get back to the treasure room."

The men turned and ran back the way they'd come. But Stefan's claustrophobia had returned with a vengeance. He'd been fighting this sense of imprisonment and confinement ever since they had left the sunlight and began prowling the narrow passageways of the temple. How he longed to see the sky again! Now on the verge of panic, he ran after the others, muttering incoherently to himself in his terror.

Finally the four men entered one of the rooms with the gold and the gems.

"Start packing these at once," Hoffmann snapped. "But we don't know where those people are. One of us will have to stay in this room while the others take the stuff to the plane."

"Then I'd better stay with the plane when you go back in the temple," Stefan said at once. "Those people came from somewhere. If they find our plane and take it, we'll lose the treasure and we'll also be stranded in this jungle."

"You're right," Hoffmann said. "But we'll take turns staying with the plane and in this room. Start packing."

Hurriedly, the men tore open their bags and took out the sacks they'd brought. Then they ran to the walls and shelves and began to rip off the gold ornaments and stuff these in their sacks. Quickly, they'd filled three of the bags with as much weight as they could handle.

"Kala, keep loading these empty sacks while we're gone," Hoffmann said, as he, Walther, and Stefan shouldered their packs and headed through the tunnel that led them to the side of the temple.

Meanwhile, just within the jungle, watching the temple through the bushes, Mark and Maria sat on the ground beside a tall tree. Through breaks in the leaves of the low bushes they could see the side of the great temple mound.

"Oh Mark, I've been praying that they'll come out soon! Before those men do."

"So have I," he said.

Mark was feeling more and more desperate. Once, several minutes before, he'd left Maria behind the edge of the jungle and had gone back to Hoffmann's plane to check the cockpit. Climbing inside, he'd made sure again that the craft was ready to fly. Then he ran back and sat down again beside her. Fervently he wished that their own plane was on this side of the temple, and not the opposite! But Mr. Daring's plane was out of their sight now, hidden from view by the temple mound, beyond their immediate reach.

We might have to fly Hoffmann's craft! he thought to himself. Quietly, he began to explain his plan to Maria, not realizing how long he was taking his gaze away from watching the temple.

Mark never saw the big man Walther come out of a tunnel, climb down to the ground, and walk quickly to Hoffmann's aircraft, carrying a heavy sack of treasure.

Suddenly Maria looked back to the temple and gasped. "Mark! Look! There are men coming out of the temple!"

Horror-struck, Mark swept his gaze to the temple. There, on a level above ground, two men had emerged from a gap in the vines. The men turned and began working on something at their feet.

"What are they doing?" Maria said.

"I don't know," he said. "But they're getting ready to climb down, I think." Then he narrowed his eyes: "There's Hoffmann."

One of the men stood up, turned their way, and tossed the end of a long rope to the ground below.

"Mark, you're right!" she said desperately. "They're coming down!"

"C'mon, Maria, we'll stay inside the bushes but we've got to beat them to that plane!"

"But Penny and David are still inside!" she said.

"I know, but we don't know whether those men saw our plane when they landed, or not. If they didn't, they might see it when they take off, and then they'd land for sure and track us down. And I just realized that we can take off now, radio Colonel Lamumba, then fly around on this side of the temple until he sends help. That way, we can distract Hoffmann and his men when David and Penny get out of the temple, too, so they'll know to climb around to the other side and take off in our plane. I think we've *got* to get in the air!"

He rose to a crouch and led her rapidly through the low bushes toward the plane some thirty yards away. When they came opposite the aircraft, Mark peered through the bushes at the men on the temple mound. "One of them's coming down on that rope!" he said. "Quick, Maria, follow me!"

Walther stowed the heavy sack in the back of the plane, climbed back out to the ground, turned, and was almost run into by Mark.

Shocked at the sudden appearance of the big man, Mark skidded to a stop. Walther grinned quickly and shot out a left jab. Desperately, Mark ducked to the side, pivoted on his right foot and swept his left leg in a vicious arc, knocking Walther's leading leg from under him.

Walther grunted in pain at the powerful blow to his knee, stumbled, and was falling when Mark pivoted again and slammed his fist twice into the big man's temple. Walther went down, sweeping out a mighty arm as he fell, and caught Mark a vicious blow in the stomach. Mark tensed his muscles just in time, but the man's powerful fist stunned him, and he doubled over in pain.

Walther staggered to his feet, and swung with his right. Mark ducked, and then kicked again at the big man's knee, knocking Walther's leg out from under him. Again, Mark struck the man's head as he fell to the ground. Walther groaned, clutched his knee, and did not get up.

"Get in the plane, Maria!" Mark cried out. She climbed in at once and jumped into the seat behind the pilot's. Mark piled into the pilot's seat and frantically searched the control panel.

"Pull that door shut, and lock it," he said, as his hands flew across the controls, "then fasten your belt!"

Swiftly Maria closed the door of the plane, then got back again into the seat behind Mark. "Mark, there are two men on the ground now, and they've got some big sacks with them."

"They're stealing the treasure, like you thought," he said. Then he was too busy turning on the engine to say more.

Standing on the ledge above the other two men, Hoffmann glanced at the plane and shouted in alarm. Just under the body of the aircraft he could see Walther's fall to the ground. Then the wings of the plane moved as people got inside.

"Someone's stealing the plane!" Hoffmann shouted in shock. "We've got to stop them!"

"Stealing my plane?" Stefan screamed, stunned. He looked up from the heavy bag he was preparing to lower down to the ground. Hoffmann had already plunged into the matted vines, and was fighting his way to the ground. Stefan dropped the sack of treasure and followed him.

The sudden roar of the aircraft's engine shocked the two men.

Horrified, Hoffmann and Stefan looked over at the plane. The engine was running and the propeller spinning.

"Grab the wing before they start moving!" Stefan screamed, reaching the ground just behind Hoffmann, and breaking into a wild run for the aircraft.

"Walther, get up!" Hoffmann called, as he too ran toward the aircraft with a wild curse.

"Grab the wing!" Stefan yelled again, as the running men closed the distance. "We'll make them go in circles till Walther gets up and yanks them out of the cockpit!"

"TAKE OFF! TAKE OFF!"

While Mark and Maria were coming ashore from the canoe, David and Penny had been standing on the narrow ledge in the dreadful darkness, waiting for Penny's leg muscle to cease cramping.

"It hurts, David," she said.

"Don't tense up!" he said quickly. "Relax as much as you can. Lean on the wall and rest a minute."

He stepped back toward her, reached his right arm around her shoulder, and held her steady against the damp wall. They waited several minutes in silence and in desperate prayer—the minutes seemed like hours to them.

"Now see if you can move your leg a little," he said.

Oh, Lord, he prayed, *Let us finish this crossing.*

Time stood still. The light in David's left hand still illumined the door in the wall across the abyss. It seemed so far away—would they ever reach it?

"It's a little better, David!" she said.

"Can you stand on it?"

"I'll try."

David waited, praying that she'd soon be able to continue the crossing. *Time's running out* he realized. *Those men could catch up with us at any moment.*

"David, I think I can walk now."

"Thank the Lord!" he said. "Let's go. Take it easy, though. Don't put much weight on that leg until you're sure it'll hold you."

At a slower pace now, they continued their laborious passage through the darkness that covered the waters and the fighting animals below them. They reached the middle of the walkway. "Easy does it, Penny," David said again, "take your time."

"It's better, David," she said.

Half step by half step they moved along the wet stone wall. Then, they were three quarters of the way across. "We're getting there, Penny!" David said. "We're closer!"

Then—an eternity later—they were only five yards away from the platform.

"Careful, Penny," David cautioned. "We can't make a mistake now, we're almost there. Easy does it."

Then David took the last step and stood on the stone platform! Reaching out, he put his arm around her shoulder. Slowly she moved her feet the last half step, and left the narrow ledge. He pulled her quickly away from the ledge and toward the door and into his arms.

"We did it, Penny! We made it!"

"Oh, David, thank the Lord!" She was crying now, with joy and relief.

"You knew the direction to take, Penny," he said. "I'd gotten turned around in that place. But we can't waste a minute—we've got to get out of here, meet Mark and Maria, and get to our plane!"

David pressed open the door—it opened easily and at once—and they entered another narrow tunnel. In less that fifty steps they came to a turn in the passage.

"I see light!" Penny exclaimed. "David, we've reached the outside!"

She was right. Before them was a vine-covered doorway through which sunlight filtered past the vines. David stuffed his flashlight in his pants pocket, and began to pull the vines apart. Now the bright sunlight almost blinded them both. Penny had tears of joy in her eyes.

"We've made it, David!" she cried happily. "Can you see Mark and Maria?"

"Not yet," he said, "but I see something strange. We're standing just above a stone chute that slopes down to the ground. And the vines seem to make a net above it. Maybe we can scramble down this. It looks like it'd be a lot easier than trying to climb down those vines."

But it wasn't easy. Slowly they worked their way downward, fighting off the falling vines that leaned on them from the vast netting that covered the temple.

"We're getting there, Penny," David said, unable to keep the excitement out of his voice. "We're almost to the ground!"

The thunder of the airplane's engine shocked them both.

"What's that?" David asked incredulously. "Our plane's on the other side of the temple."

"It must be Hoffmann's plane, then," Penny said. "That's the only way he and his men could have gotten to this place."

"Quick, Penny, let's get to the ground. But we'll stay inside these vines until we can see what's going on."

They scrambled the short distance down the steeply sloping chute until they were almost to the ground. Still crouching behind the thick cover, David worked a hole in the vegetation and peered out. The plane's engine was roaring now.

"It's going to take off!" he said.

Frantically, he pulled the vines apart and searched the ground between the temple mound and the jungle. And there, to his left, he was shocked to see two men running toward another private plane. The running men had almost reached it when the aircraft began to move, heading away to his left. Mark's blond head was visible in the cockpit.

Bouncing along the ground, the plane pulled away from the running men. Now David saw a third man lying on the ground near the edge of the bushes.

"That's Mark in the cockpit," David exclaimed. "He's going to take off. Quick Penny, we've got to get to the ground!"

The two scrambled frantically through the matted vines, down the stone chute that led to the ground. Finally they reached the end, and came out into the open.

To their left, beyond the temple, just this side of the underbrush, the plane was bouncing on the ground as it made a tight turn back toward them. Hoffmann and another man were running desperately after it, and had almost reached the turning craft, hoping to grab the wings and spin it around and pull out Mark and Maria.

"He's coming back," David said excitedly. "He's got to take off this way, along the side of the temple. Quick, we'll run out and meet him!"

They ran out into the cleared space beside the temple and began waving at the aircraft. It had turned now, and as the two running men grabbed desperately for the wing tips, Mark gunned the engine. The plane began to move toward David and Penny, slowly at first, then faster.

Frantically Stefan grabbed for the tip of the plane's wing as it passed, but it tore through his grasp. With a cry of despair, he threw himself to the ground.

But Hoffmann didn't give up! He failed to grab the wing, but with a strength fed by rage and implacable determination he raced after the aircraft, hoping he could grab the tail and force the plane to swerve and stop.

Inside the cockpit of the plane, Mark spotted Penny and David. "There they are!" he cried out to Maria. "They made it! We'll pick them up and get away at last. Oh,

Maria, we're almost out of here!" He began to slow the plane.

Neither Mark nor Maria could see how close the running Hoffmann was to the taxiing aircraft. It had pulled ahead of him for a moment, but then he began to close the distance as Mark slowed the aircraft to pick up David and Penny who were running toward him.

For the moment, Penny and David couldn't see Hoffmann either, for his body was hidden by the fuselage of the approaching aircraft.

"Mark's almost here," David cried exultantly. "Just a few more feet, Penny, and we'll meet him!"

Suddenly Penny stumbled; her leg had cramped again, and she cried out to David as she fell to the ground.

David halted, stooped, and picked her up in his arms.

"Oh David, I'm so sorry," she said, as she put her arms around his neck.

"We'll make it," he said grimly. "Hold tight." He turned to meet the approaching aircraft.

He met Hoffmann instead.

The grim and determined man raced around the slowing aircraft, yelled with vicious satisfaction as he saw the two, and swerved to attack David.

David, heart in throat, barely had time to place Penny on the ground and move away from her when the running espionage agent threw his body at him in a flying kick, feet ready to strike like the point of an arrow aimed at the boy's head.

David threw himself to the side with a jerk as the man flew by him, the striking feet just missing him. Hoffmann landed like a cat, and raced back toward David.

David set himself in a fighting stance, ready to parry kick or blow, but was unprepared for the speed with which his adversary struck at his head with a roundhouse kick. David's hands barely deflected the man's foot as he ducked away, when Hoffmann continued his body's lightning-fast turn, and struck at him again with another kick.

David's hands flew to protect his head, and caught the man's foot, but the force of Hoffmann's kick knocked him sprawling. He scrambled to his feet in desperate haste, just in time to step aside from the fastest front-kick he'd ever faced. But he got in a blow at the German's head as Hoffmann recovered, and this stunned the man for a moment.

Then Hoffmann faked a kick to the head again, and slammed it instead into David's ribs. Grunting with pain, David doubled over. *This man's too fast!* he realized. *I'll never stop all his kicks!*

Even as this dread thought raced through his mind, David's training was taking over. As Hoffmann moved to attack again, David pivoted on his back foot, leaned back with his body as his other foot swept forward, then whipped his hips around to the right. His lead foot now swept sideways into Hoffmann's leg, knocking him sprawling to the ground.

But David couldn't reach the falling man in time to hit him as he fell. He had to back off as the man scrambled to his feet and moved to attack again.

Mark, meanwhile, had pulled the plane to a stop, wondering why David and Penny hadn't reached the door and jumped in. Maria's cry froze his heart.

"Penny's fallen, and a man's fighting David!" she cried, peering back through the plane's window.

Mark reached for the door and as he did so Maria cried out again. "There's another man running toward us from the temple!"

"I've got to get Penny," he said, jumping out of the plane.

Hoffmann attacked again, faking a blow to David's face, but kicking instead. David stepped away just in time, but then closed at once and slammed his fist into Hoffmann's face, breaking the man's nose.

With a cry of rage and pain, Hoffmann stumbled back. Then he attacked again, so fast that David could only block the kick with his shoulder. David was thrown to the ground, but he rolled over and came to his feet just in time to slap aside Hoffmann's thrust-kick with his hand. Instantly he kicked out and struck Hoffmann in the ribs; the man fell to his knees, gasping in pain from a broken rib.

Mark reached them then, scooped up Penny in his arms, and raced with her back to the cockpit.

"C'mon, David," Mark yelled over the noise of the plane's engine, "get in."

Penny climbed in, Mark jumped in after her, and David, limping and bruised, climbed in last, closing and locking the door.

"You're hurt!" Maria exclaimed.

"I'm okay," he said. "Let's go!"

Mark hands flew again over the controls and the plane began to move. "I'll taxi around the temple, and back to our plane," he said, over the increased noise of the engine.

The plane gathered speed just as Walther had come to his feet and began to run toward them. Hoffmann struggled to get up, and hurried over as Kala joined them and raced to the plane, trying to grab a wing - then threw himself desperately to the side as Mark swerved the craft and its deadly swirling propeller toward him.

Mark gunned the engine again and steadied the plane on course, pouring on more fuel as the plane bounced across the ground. Then the craft reached the end of the temple mound. Mark slowed again, turned the plane to the right, and swept out of sight of the pursuing men. Taxiing around the temple, he turned right again and headed for Jim Daring's parked Cessna.

"We're ahead of them!" he shouted. "David, can you jump in our plane when we reach it. We can't leave those men a way to get out of here!"

"Yes," David said. Bruised and bleeding, he was gasping for breath. "Yes, I can."

"We'll keep taxiing to the edge of the jungle, then turn and take off back this way," Mark said. "Watch out for those men trying to grab the edge of the wings, and turn the plane in circles!"

"I will," David replied.

Mark slowed Hoffmann's plane as they approached the Cessna. David leaped out as it was still moving, and ran, limping, over to the Cessna. Mark gunned the engine of Hoffmann's craft and moved away to give David room to bring the Cessna back out of the trees. Then he stopped and waited for David.

Oh Lord, Mark prayed, *let David get that plane started without any trouble, before those men reach us!*

David was as experienced a pilot as he was, Mark knew. Still, David was hurt, and anything could go wrong. He prayed that Hoffmann's men had not found and sabotaged the Cessna. He and the girls watched anxiously as David got into the plane's cockpit and readied the craft for flight.

Then to their vast relief, they saw the Cessna's propellers turn over! Exhaust shot from under the engine, and the plane shook under the increasing power.

"Let's go!" Mark yelled out the window to David.

"There comes Hoffmann!" Maria cried out, as she caught sight of Hoffmann's gang coming around the north end of the temple mound and towards the planes, running desperately to stop them before they got up enough speed to take off.

David watched Mark taxi Hoffmann's plane down their narrow landing strip, then he released the Cessna's brakes, pulled it out from under the trees and followed Mark past the temple mound. Mark stopped Hoffmann's craft when he got close to the trees, and turned it around, facing the Cessna. David stopped, turned the Cessna in a one hundred eighty degree turn, put on power for take-off and headed directly toward the four men running frantically toward them.

It was a very near thing. Hoffmann and his men were just not close enough to safely grab the wingtips of David's plane, and they scattered like a flock of chickens before a charging dog. The Cessna, picking up speed each moment, roared past them, lifted off and soared into the sky. Mark, Maria, and Penny, in Hoffmann's craft, took off right behind David.

Mark flew up beside the Cessna and the four happy teens yelled and waved at each other as they flew away.

Helplessly, the stranded men below shook their fists at the disappearing craft, and hurled useless curses into the air. Suddenly, Hoffmann spotted a herd of wild pigs rushing angrily out of the bush—the animals had picked up their scent at the far end of the temple mound, and were coming their way, angered at the noise of the planes soaring above them. Horrified, he yelled to his men, and they dashed desperately toward the back end of the temple, heading for the stream that came out from under the mound.

The wild pigs had been peacefully sleeping when they'd been jolted awake by the noise of the two airplanes. Enraged, they now heard the frightened yelling of Hoffmann and his men. Their feeble eyes could not see well at that distance, but they could hear, and they could smell the scent of the men who had run around the temple mound - and they didn't like what they smelled. Swiftly the herd broke into a run, their sharp tusks gleaming as they picked up speed, snorting with deadly menace as they followed the scent and the cries of the frantically fleeing *would-be* thieves.

It was a desperate chase. The wild pigs almost caught them. Hoffmann and his men reached the bank of the narrow rushing water just a few feet ahead of the lethal gleaming tusks and dived in head first. The angered pigs pulled to a sudden stop at the bank, grunting with frustration, milling around in anger.

In the middle of the narrow river, the men treaded water, amazed at their sudden escape.

Then Stefan screamed: "Crocodiles!"

Frantically, the four thieves swam for the other bank.

REST AT LAST

David wasn't sure if it was the light through the window curtains - or the aroma of the muffins - that had awakened him, so he lay still for a few moments while he tried to figure this out. He considered going back to sleep—they'd all been exhausted when they'd flown home the day before. But the smell of the muffins prevailed. He got up and dressed quickly.

Strolling into the kitchen, he found Mrs. Daring taking another batch of muffins out of the oven as she whistled a cheerful tune.

"Hi," she said cheerfully. "Have a muffin. There's a plateful on the table."

"Thanks," he said gratefully, helping himself.

"How'd you sleep, David?" she asked. Her blue eyes sparkled as she watched him dig into one of the muffins. This boy was like a son to her husband and herself, and she was grateful to have him and Maria and her own children safely home.

"Great," he replied around a mouthful, "I really got a rest. Where's everybody?"

"Penny was here a minute ago. I think she went to wake Maria."

But then Penny came in, pretty and bright-eyed in her light blue robe. "Hi," she said cheerfully. "Finally got tired of sleeping your life away?"

"Wait a minute," he protested, taking another muffin. "I've been studying and meditating since before dawn. But no one else was up, so I went back to bed to meditate some more."

"I bet you did," she said. "Where's Mark?"

"In dreamland," he said. "I try to set him an example of diligence and industry, but so far it hasn't worked. He's still sleeping. I worry about him, in fact."

"Well, Maria and I have been up for hours, just waiting for you two to recover from the exertion of flying those planes home. Honestly, David, what could be easier than sitting in a comfortable seat and steering a small airplane?" She sat at the kitchen table and looked up at him with a pitying expression, struggling not to laugh.

"Up for hours?" her mother exclaimed with a laugh. "Penny Daring! What a whopper! Tell David the truth—you just got up five minutes ago!"

David groaned and rolled his eyes in mock despair. "Mrs. Daring, please tell this young lady that she and her female companion were rescued from dreadful danger by two valiant knights. Explain to her that valiant knights have got to have a lot of rest after they've rescued maidens.

I mean, they've got to get ready to save them in their next adventure."

"There will be no 'next adventure' for you young man—or for the others either!" Mrs. Daring said emphatically. "I've been horrified at the dangers you all have encountered this summer. Week after week you've been in dreadful peril. If your and Maria's parents had had any idea of what you would be getting into, they would never have let you come here. You four will stay around this nice house for the remainder of your visit, you will enjoy our pool, and you'll have fun right here, where it's safe!"

David saw that she was getting worked up about this. She and her husband really did feel terrible that the young people had been exposed to the dangers they'd encountered everywhere they'd gone.

"Yes, Ma'am," he said quickly. "That sure suits me fine. I'm tired of adventures. I want to swim. And listen to my new Vivaldi CDs. And we haven't looked through Mark's telescope all summer."

Penny came over and stood before David as he was sitting in the chair. Her face suddenly became solemn. "How many times did you save my life yesterday, David?"

He didn't know how to reply at first. Slowly his face got red. Then he answered. "Penny, you knew the way out of that temple and I'd gotten lost. You saved both of us!"

"Hush, David. Maria told me how you jumped down into the room when that horrible snake was coming toward me. And you pulled me away from that falling wall when it fell. And you held me when my leg cramped up on that dreadful narrow ledge. And you carried me when I fell outside the temple."

She held out her hands, and he took them in his. Now his face was really red.

"Oh, David," she said, looking down at him, with the strangest expression in her eyes. She didn't know what else to say. Neither did he.

"Is everybody up but me?" Maria asked brightly, as she entered the room. Like Penny, she too wore her robe.

Quickly David released Penny's hands. "Not Mark," he replied. "He'll sleep until eleven, probably." His face was still red.

"David, it *is* eleven," Mrs. Daring laughed.

"So here you all are," Mark said suddenly, bursting into the room. Like David, he wore slacks and a polo shirt. "I've been wandering all over the yard, meditating on life, thinking deep thoughts, wondering when you'd all finally come to life and get out of bed."

Everyone laughed at that. Penny then turned to her mom. "What can I do to help?" she asked.

"You can set the table, Penny," Mrs. Daring replied. "The eggs are almost ready, the juice is poured, and the muffins are done. We're about ready to feed you folks a rather late breakfast."

Mr. Daring came in just as they'd finished eating and he was beaming.

"Well, you young folks will be glad to hear this," he announced, pulling out a chair and helping himself to a muffin.

"Hear what, Dad?" Penny asked.

"Colonel Lamumba and his men flew out to the temple when you radioed them from the air, Mark. They attacked in helicopters, landed, and captured Hoffmann and his three men. Wild pigs had chased them into the stream, and they'd jumped into the water to escape. Then the crocodiles had chased them into the trees on the other bank. They were in terrible shape. Not only that, the Colonel's men found a treasure that those crooks were going to steal."

"You mean they actually captured Hoffmann and his gang?" Penny asked, almost in disbelief. "Can it be true?"

"It sure can be true!" her dad replied. "Hoffmann, a big man named Walther, a pilot, and an African named Kala. Walther and Kala were captured before, after chasing you young folks on the river, but they had escaped a few weeks ago. But they're all locked up now."

"But why did Hoffmann come to that temple, Dad?" Mark asked. "I mean, how did he learn there was treasure there?"

"They learned about the temple through a spy in Colonel Lamumba's office. And they guessed that there'd be a treasure there. But they didn't count on you four being there too."

Her dad's face beamed with pleasure as he looked at Penny. "They have really captured Hoffmann at last, honey, and the Colonel assures me that he and his men will be locked up for a long, long time." He grinned with delight. "This is a clean sweep. Those men began all our troubles at the beginning of the summer, and now they're caught. You kids have done a wonderful job."

"Actually, Dad, we were mostly just trying to get away." Mark had the strangest feeling that he'd told his dad this once before.

Jim Daring was beside himself with pleasure. "Colonel Lamumba said there are so many charges against Hoffmann for his criminal activities in this country that he'll be put away for life! He certainly won't trouble you any more."

"And last night Maria's folks said she could visit us for two more weeks," Penny exclaimed brightly. "We'll see that you have lots of fun, Maria."

"Hey," David said eagerly, "when I called my folks yesterday, I asked if Mark and Penny and Maria could come visit us in the States two weeks from now. Can we plan on this?"

Mrs. Daring spoke quickly. "Thanks for inviting them, David, and your parents suggested the same thing to me. But Jim and I will have to think about that. After all, they've been away from home all summer."

"What about next month, then?" David asked quickly. He felt Penny's gaze on him, and his face got red.

"We'll see, David," Mr. Daring laughed. "I know they'd love to do that."

Later that evening the four teens took a stroll down the road from the Darings house. The soft moonlight fell on them as they passed through the shadows of the tall trees.

"I hate to think of your going back, David," Penny said, as they walked side by side behind Mark and Maria.

"I do too. But I know it's time I got back to my family."

"What a summer it's been." she said, looking up at him. She was wearing the light blue dress she'd worn their last night in Cairo with Mr. and Mrs. Froede—she knew David liked it. As they walked, the moonlight bathed her in its golden glow and David was entranced. He thought of all that they'd been through together.

"The Lord sure kept us from a lot of harm these past weeks, Penny," he said.

"Do you think you'll run into adventures back in Alabama?" she asked, a twinkle in her eyes.

"I sure hope not. I've had enough excitement to last me a long time."

"So have we," Mark broke in from ahead of them. "And about your leaving, David, much as I'll miss you, it still might be a good thing."

"Mark," Penny exclaimed, shocked at her brother's words.

"I mean the danger he's brought with him, Penny. Look how peaceful a life we lead—and have led—until this guy breezed in from Alabama. But from the minute he landed in Africa we've been on one long wild roller-coaster ride after another, with hair-raising escapes. I thought I'd never have to stop saving him from the trouble he got into."

"Mark," David protested, "I'm the one who longs for peace and quiet. And if it hadn't been for me, you'd have been long gone. Man, I rescued you from more scrapes…!"

Penny and Maria laughed at the boys as they bantered.

On the way home, David spoke quietly to Penny. "It's been a lot of danger, but I'll miss you."

"I'll miss you, too" she replied, smiling up at him.

She stumbled suddenly. David reached quickly for her hand and steadied her.